## PRAISE FOR *A BRUTAL DESIGN*

"Part utopia, part dystopia, Zachary C. Solomon's smart, accomplished novel wears its ambitions proudly on its sleeves. *A Brutal Design* is attentive to the brutalities of history even as it trains its eyes on the future. It's an engrossing and powerful debut."

—Joshua Henkin, author of *Morningside Heights*

"Through its magnetic and momentous descent into the darkness that lurks beneath the surface of the desert utopia Duma, *A Brutal Design* convincingly depicts the insidious way that ideological oppression can seep into the world around us. There were moments in Solomon's novel that truly frightened me, and yet, like its narrator, Samuel Zelnik, I found myself obsessively compelled to uncover its mysteries. This is a haunting, thought-provoking novel that shows a place where the senseless meets reality."

—Gabe Habash, author of *Stephen Florida*

"*A Brutal Design* is a deft blend of sci-fi, noir, and a dash of Sebald that examines our yearning for utopia. It is propelled by unease, yet funny and beautiful, too. Once I started reading it, I could not stop."

—Erin Somers, author of *Stay Up With Hugo Best*

"With searing prose and breakneck pace, *A Brutal Design* delves into the terrifying and prescient intersections of art, fascism, and belief in one's ideals. An uncompromising portrait of the human psyche and overflowing with philosophical depth, Solomon's debut impresses and stays with you, long after you finish the book."

—Soon Wiley, author of *When We Fell Apart*

"*A Brutal Design* is an absurdist, falling-down-the-rabbit-hole adventure packed with dark mysteries, startling images, and surreal encounters. At the same time, this book is keenly political, rich with implications for both the past and the future. Through his evocation of the ostensibly utopian city of Duma, Zachary C. Solomon deftly explores the relationships between art, bureaucracy, violence, and political control. This is an exhilarating and boldly original debut."

—Helen Phillips, author of *The Need*

"With commanding intelligence and dystopian foresight, *A Brutal Design* secures Zachary C. Solomon's place in the world of letters with a voice steeped in history, literature, art, and philosophy, and maturity beyond its years. His taut, elegantly written, and exquisitely bleak novel presciently pits fascism against dwindling humanity, asking: Do we value life little enough that we'd exchange it for "advancement and comfort"? This is a haunting, sinister, and brilliant debut."

—Sara Lippmann, author of *Lech*

# A BRUTAL DESIGN

# A BRUTAL DESIGN

ZACHARY C. SOLOMON

LANTERNFISH PRESS

PHILADELPHIA

A BRUTAL DESIGN

Copyright © 2023 by Zachary C. Solomon

Lanternfish Press
P.O. Box 34569
Philadelphia, PA 19101
lanternfishpress.com

Cover Design: Kimberly Glyder
Cover Image: Berenice Melis
Illustrations: Basking shark photograph by Alex Mustard. Used with permission.

Printed in the United States of America.
27 26 25 24 23    1 2 3 4 5

Library of Congress Control Number: 2023934055
Print ISBN: 978-1-941360-81-1
Digital ISBN: 978-1-941360-82-8

*For my mother and my sister.*

# ONE

I WAS ON THE VERGE when the train pulled in at half past three. For hours I'd sat with my face pressed against the glass, fogging it with my breath through the day of graceless, nauseous rocking toward the north, then far to the east, and finally south. I was tired and queasy and had been punished severely for teaching my benchmate, a mere hour into our eleven-hour journey, the English phrase *long-distance telephone* at her pleading. She had practiced it ceaselessly, with torturous intention, as the world changed beyond the window, grew harsher, filthier, more—then less—industrial, as we passed through the city, suburbs, exurbs, countryside, and into the infinite steppe, well beyond the cessation of electrical poles and industry markers, until, at last, the station appeared in the distance. The people in my compartment began to stir, to collect their belongings from the overhead. My neighbor swallowed audibly, straightened her skirt, and looked at me. *Long-distance telephone, long-distance telephone, long-distance telephone.*

# A BRUTAL DESIGN

I was hopeful for myself, but not for her.

We disembarked. I stood to the side, away from the rest of the travelers, breathing the sandy air and waiting for the porter to emerge by the train's sleek, streamlined beak. He appeared through a swirl of steam and got to work unloading suitcases onto the wooden platform. I let the others collect theirs first while I looked around. The station, an imposing concrete wave, stood in a bleak expanse of dry, green brush. The air was hot, the soil red clay, fine and dusty. The others from my compartment—businessmen and businesswomen in quickly dirtying suits or jumpsuits, wearing flats—found their way inside to make their calls. I waited until only one bag remained, figuring it had to be mine. I hadn't been allowed to do the packing myself. I'd been supplied the bag.

Down the tracks by the rear of the train, people were still cascading from the second-class cars, dropping their valises and blinking into the sunshine, a mass of thread-bare gray and brown coats groping for direction. Coats in this weather meant they weren't traveling on a roundtrip ticket. Meant they were wearing everything they owned, for whatever contingencies life might thrust at them.

I wondered why I wasn't among them. Why I'd been ticketed a first-class berth.

A short man in a pinstriped suit and vest stood by the station holding a white sign with my name on it. He had taken pains to add serifs to each letter. No one had ever held a sign for me before. I felt exposed and quickly flushed with sweat. I nodded at him, then took out a hand-kerchief and wiped my brow. I was a profuse sweater and forever embarrassed by it. The porter placed my duffel at my feet. I patted my pockets for a tip.

As the driver approached, I saw that the suit he wore was made of wool and that his socks were wool, too, visible beneath pant legs that had been hemmed too high. Wool in this weather. I felt bad for him, a man who had to sweat like me. I thought about taking a stand if they made me wear a uniform like that. I reminded myself that I had agreed to come here, that I had to stand by my decision. I chastised myself for complaining. But then again, is there really a decision if the alternative is simply intolerable?

He had puffy cheeks, the driver, and a thick eyebrow that wormed when he spoke, though he was handsome, if a little haggard. It wasn't a stretch to picture him gulping down a stein of ale or wearing overalls on some stormy quay. I placed him in his fifties. His teeth were straight and bleached.

Though I tried to resist, the driver took my bag and placed it gently in the trunk of his car, a functional, sexless hybrid that had seen cleaner days. He then opened the back door for me, but I sidestepped him and went to climb into the passenger side in front. He rushed to open that door too, the two of us doing an awkward dance of decorum. He was intent on following the instructions of his position and I was intent on showing him that I wouldn't be a burden. I sensed little room for improvisation in his life, even the kind of friendly corner-cutting a bureaucrat might do for a friend he sees in the back of the line. He introduced himself as Henry and apologized for the mess.

# A BRUTAL DESIGN

Cassettes and maps and lighters and a gold-plated tire pressure gauge lay in the footwell. But no dust.

We pulled out of the station parking lot and joined up with the highway. In the side mirror, I glimpsed a few of the second-class passengers piling into a big, industrial van. I thought maybe they would be taken where I was being taken—but if that were the case, why no signs for them? I couldn't shake the feeling that if it weren't for some unfair advantage, I would have been among them. The hybrid struggled to catch up to cruising speed and cars overtook us viciously, each one sending our little car bobbing. Earth spread out on either side in a crenelated landscape, farms demarcated by rolling hills, grain elevators, water towers, windmills chopping air. It was easy to see from the elevated road the plan of the countryside, the towering housing blocks with curved balconies arranged in clusters around airy plazas, the brutalist municipal structures, the fountains and playgrounds and regional flags—architecture not so different from home. Stunning to see so many people at once, or the evidence of them. It was like I could feel the presence of hundreds of thousands of lives as we bumped up the road to the south.

I was trying to figure out whether it would be impolite to ask Henry a question when he spoke.

"You're going to like it," he said. "You're going to like everything about it."

I wasn't sure if he was referring to the country, the region, or our destination. He drove carefully, hands on twelve and two, his eyes darting up to the rearview every ten seconds. We passed tailgaters whose cars sported bumper stickers written in a language I couldn't identify. Muzak drifted through the car's tinny speakers, a reedy, vaguely melodic vamp.

"There's a particular kind of genius to it," he continued. "An actual brilliance." He tapped his right temple with a pointer finger, as if to show where the brilliance was kept. "You'll see. When you walk around the campus, how easy it is to navigate. To find your office, groceries, to get to the athletic complex. Intuitive geography. You know where to go without knowing where to go. You'll see. It's very simple. Elegant."

I asked how long he'd lived in Duma.

"Since the start. Since it was a little baby settlement. And now it's all grown up. When I first got to Duma, there was only a handful of concrete blocks in a circle in the middle of the desert."

"What made you come out here?"

"It was so long ago I can't remember. I'll let you know if I do." He smiled, glanced at the rearview, adjusted the angle. "So what's your preference?"

"For what?"

"What you want to do. What you're hoping for. You know, a job."

Henry was requesting a level of transparency from me that I wasn't entirely comfortable with. I was exhausted, bled utterly dry by the long journey, my senses dulled to nubs. I decided I would just repeat what I'd been told.

"They said they needed an architect."

Henry risked a glance at me and the car drifted a bit onto the shoulder. I squeezed the armrest. I hated driving, or being driven, or really any kind of locomotion. I'd get carsick, seasick, airsick. I got dizzy on sidewalks.

"Very unusual," said Henry. "Good for you. But don't get your hopes up."

"Why not?"

"I was a dentist before I got here. Great, they said, we could use a driver. Now I'm a driver."

"They specifically told me I'd be designing buildings," I said. "I'm doing my graduate studies in architecture right now. My uncle already lives in Duma, as a chemical engineer."

"Oh, yeah? How do you know?"

"He sent me a letter."

Henry roared with laughter. "Good luck with your studies," he said.

His dismissal made me despair. I closed my eyes to the sunlight that strobed through an oasis of trees and thought about how I would fight back against the bureaucrats. I had been told—and this had been corroborated by Uncle's letter—that I would help design buildings with Uncle's letter—that I would help design buildings necessary for the growth of Duma. I was told the settlement was nearly ready to enter a new phase, that it would be expanding infrastructure to accommodate an increased population, that the experiment was showing signs of success. If the ethos behind this place was a progressive one, and if it truly was an attempt at communal, collaborative, socialist living as I'd been told, then I wanted to contribute. I wanted to help prove that the man my parents had raised me to be could find purchase in a kind and fair society. And I wanted to do it through architecture. To show that buildings, like governments, could be democratic: bastions of equality, dismantlers of hierarchies.

I wondered how Uncle V. was getting along out here without Mela and Elam to take care of him. Without me to push around. I listened to the car radio and remembered a time, not so long past, when I was working at the kitchen table in our house on Alizabet Street. That horrid table. One leg two inches shorter than the other three. That table was the totem at the center of our poverty. We were poorer than we'd ever been, our meal tickets yielding less and less, and our house was haunted by the mysterious stench of eggs despite the citywide shortage. I sometimes wondered if the odor emanated from Uncle V. himself, given that he had stopped bathing some time before—in rueful protest, I supposed, of the continuation of his regrettable existence. He had been back from jail for a few weeks by then and had not recovered any of his character. I had yet to learn why he'd been to jail in the first place. He would tell Mela and Elam the story shortly thereafter. I would learn it from them shortly after that.

About that table. For a time we used dried newspaper pulp to prop up its stunted leg. The pulp lasted a week, maybe nine days, then Mela or Elam would deliver a bit more of the stuff. They got it from the local paper crusher, in exchange for who knows what. They were always taking care of us—of you, Uncle—for reasons that escaped me for a long time. I didn't know then what I know now: that I owed you a debt of gratitude as immense and imposing as the perilous Mount Elbrus—and as proficient at claiming souls.

# A BRUTAL DESIGN

They were over, both Mela and Elam, that day I was working at the table. At least one of them was at our house on any given day, typically to remind you to bathe and eat, to be nice to your nephew. I couldn't take care of you. I didn't want to. You had always made it clear that it was you who had to take care of *me*. And that I should never forget it. And that I should always feel a responsibility for it.

You had come in from the outside and stood in the open doorway, watching me. Behind you, the street glistened from a morning rain shower. The smell of sulfur wafted in. My plans were scattered about me on the tilted table, my drafting pencil rolling over and over to the edge. The humidity was turning my tracing paper to mush.

"The immigrant toils and toils," said Uncle. "He toils forever and never sees nothing for his efforts."

"Not you," I said. "You don't toil and toil."

"I'm not an immigrant. I was born here. In this very house." He spat dryly onto the wooden floorboards, eliciting a reprimand from Mela.

"I'm not an immigrant either," I said.

"Stop your working, then. Your time is almost up."

"*Our* time," I said.

"What is it you're working on anyway? So diligent and studious."

I was in the fourth and final year, I hoped, of my graduate studies in architecture. My thesis lay before me on the crooked table. But I wouldn't show him. He would never understand. In fact, he would be angry with me for it, furious even; he would find it indignant, pretentious, a futile attempt to make meaning out of a meaningless past. I didn't want him to blemish it, or worse. Tracing paper was hard to come by.

"Leave him be," said Mela. "Let him hope." She meant it as a positive reinforcement but it came out like something you would say around a naïve child.

"I bet you," said Uncle. "Watch: your university gates will be closed to you by month's end."

I couldn't afford to think that far ahead. I had to deal with what was in front of me. And my thesis was in front of me. I kept drafting, using my set square and my French curve in equal measure, chasing equilibrium between right angles and curves. I heard him coming closer and instinctively covered my papers. But instead of poking his nose in, he let a few sticky cheese pastries fall onto the table.

Elam rushed over. "How?" He plied one with his thumbs, sniffed the glucose. "They're still fresh?" A string of sugar thinned and then broke between his fingers.

Uncle shrugged. "I have a method."

"Theft? Theft isn't a method. Recklessness is your method."

He showed his teeth, still maddeningly white.

"You'll go back to jail," said Elam, but Uncle was already halfway toward his bedroom.

The three of us each ate a pastry, but there was no enjoyment, since the food was tainted by Uncle's parlor trickery, his fake kindness that came at his own expense, so that we had to feel guilty about the happiness he gave us. He wanted us to be pleased by his actions, though they were the actions of a villain. No one asked him to martyr himself, yet he chose that path anyway. And since he'd stepped in to raise me when no one else would or could, I had no choice but to be thankful to him.

Henry cleared his throat, pulled his collar away from his neck, and grimaced.

"Did you ever take those vocational tests?" he asked me. "Or are they before your time? The ones where you filled out a questionnaire and then a machine would tell you what you should be when you grow up."

"Did yours say 'driver'?"

This time, when Henry laughed, his shoulders pumped up and down and his head shrank into his jacket. "It told me I was going to work in finance." He chuckled again. "Me. Finance."

"Are you bad at math?"

"Are you kidding me? I'm great at math. When I was a kid, I was the top of my class. Algebra, geometry, trigonometry, physics, calculus. Name it, I solved it." Henry shifted in his seat to unstick the shirt from his back. I could see the shadow of sweat the seatbelt had left across his chest.

The way he spoke made me think he might be pulling my leg. It sounded so odd to list the fields of mathematics out like that. He waited for me to ask the next question, which I did: why he hadn't pursued the field, if he had the aptitudes.

He was ready with his answer. "Have you ever thought about how utterly inane money is? Really, truly, thought about it?"

"I haven't."

He held up his hand and extended his fingers, then lowered one with each punctuated remark. "You do a job. You get paid. You turn around and spend the money. The money swims in circles. It winds up at your job." When he ran out of fingers, he pulled his hand into a fist and moved it like he was slamming a table. "You do the job. You get the same money. You spend it on the same things. The money just circulates. It's like how the water you flush in the toilet goes into a plant where they clean it—supposedly—and then you drink that same water at the water fountain in the park."

He went on like this for twenty minutes. I was grateful for his self-sustaining monologue. I didn't have it in me to collaborate on a conversation when Henry was very clearly happy to have one by himself. I was too worn out from the noxious, interminable traveling. I had taken two trains for a total of fourteen hours. I sat facing the direction of our progress and didn't once look at a sheet of text, lest I want to throw up.

Henry had an accent, probably New York or Chicago or Boston, one of those American cities with a lot of famous, boastful personalities, where people spoke in a loud and friendly and hammering sort of way. Cities incapable of whispering. But Henry didn't look American. I pegged him as hailing from somewhere in sub-Saharan Africa, maybe. I wondered if I'd ever get to see New York myself, after all the hours I'd poured into studying its degenerate architecture in the dark—from books I'd sent for from faraway libraries, picked up in obscure alleys, and hidden in the folds of sheets and sweaters. Henry droned on. His voice began to lull me and I worried that if I fell asleep, he would think I was being rude, would take advantage of me. But the heat through the windshield, the sun on my corduroy trousers, the haze of the highway and the repetition of the countryside, the reverberations of the road—I had no choice but to succumb.

We were still driving when I woke up, still rumbling down the highway. Water vapor poured out of the air conditioning vents. I put my hand in front of one and watched the vapor snake around my fingers. I felt disoriented and nauseated. My mouth was dry and my head responded disapprovingly to the imperfections of the road. And the music had changed. It was no longer Muzak but some kind of ambient water sounds, little staccato blips and glitches and swirls. I closed my eyes and visualized each sound as a green or blue node on a grid. Music meant to calm the worker into efficiency—but I liked it; like I was meant to.

Henry reached his right arm behind him to the pouch on the back of his seat and brought forth a small plastic water bottle. I drank it down in one go, renewing the parched landscape of my mouth. I thanked him and asked if we were close.

"We're at Exit 470. When we hit Exit 500, we'll be seven-eighths of the way," said Henry, demonstrating his mathematical acumen. "Do you need to go to the bathroom?"

I did, now that he asked. But I told him I could wait another eighth of time.

The landscape had changed while I napped. We were passing through lightly undulating hills. The martian earth was now spotted with inviting pockets of grass and copses of richly red-brown cypress trees. The settlements, the farms organized around metropolitan areas, the neat roadwork—they had all disappeared. Nothing but raw terra firma now. I'd never seen anything like it. Where I came from, the land beyond the town limits was crowded with collectivized farms and famished peasantry. There was nowhere to be alone.

I missed it painfully.

The sun was setting on my side of the window, blinding me. A band of orange light sliced the car. I rotated the vanity mirror so it blocked the ray but I could still feel a strip on the lower half of my face. I rubbed my chin where the light touched it. I needed a shave.

"I know I'm not supposed to ask," said Henry, "but where are you from?"

"You're not supposed to ask?"

He pursed his lips and moved his head ambivalently. "It's one of their main things. You don't know anyone's story and no one knows yours. You come from nowhere just like everyone else. It eliminates prejudice, evens the field, et cetera, et cetera."

That didn't make a lot of sense to me, given what I knew about the people who'd sent me—they were people with origin fixations. I asked Henry if the strategy worked.

"It does for me," he said. "No one knows where I'm from."

I looked at Henry and put my hand on my chin. "United States, obviously," I said. I made a show of studying him. "Chicago."

He chuckled amiably. "Lyon," he said. "France."

This was an unpleasant surprise. I hadn't even been close. "It's so easy to think you know something," I said. His English was perfect. I wondered if he'd modeled it after American television like some of my classmates. I never watched the stuff myself, and I'm sure he could tell—my own English was nothing special. "You can't ever know anything," I said, dismayed.

"Hey, cheer up, pal. It's no big deal."

"The other day I was sitting in the park," I said. "I was on a blanket by a little, scummy pond we have, reading a novel. I had sunglasses on my head. I was in the shade and it was cloudy, you know, so I didn't need them. I had them perched on top of my head like this." I mimed the motion. "I know the expression."

"I was reading on the blanket and I noticed, from the corner of my eye, a man striding toward me. A man with shaggy blond hair in a messy part. He was wearing a baggy shirt and baggy jeans. He had a bit of a belly. He was listening to music. Just cutting through the park, following desire lines, ignoring the pavement."

"So what'd he do? Pull a gun on you?"

I looked at Henry. "How did you know?"

He shrugged. "It's where stories go."

"He didn't have a gun," I said. "He walked up to me, so close that I thought he was going to step on my blanket, nodded at me, and said, 'Cool glasses, mister.' And that was it. Then he walked away."

We were both quiet for a moment. Saying this out loud made me feel stupid, but I couldn't finish the story prematurely.

Finally, I went on. "I was so convinced he was going to pull out a pistol and slaughter me that by the time he'd gone, I thought my heart was giving out. I knew it so deeply, so personally, that he was going to shoot me. I knew it intuitively. To the point where it was almost disappointing when he didn't. I couldn't stop thinking about it. I guess I'm still thinking about it. Why would he compliment my sunglasses, if I weren't wearing them? They were on my head. The fact that I wasn't wearing them made his compliment seem so sinister to me. And why did he walk up so close to me? He didn't have to. He was doing this to intimidate me, right? To antagonize me. To spy on me."

"To spy on you?"

"It's what people do where I live."

"How old was this guy, you think?"

"Fourteen. Maybe fifteen."

Henry looked at me with something like disgust. "That's not a *man*," he said. "That's a *kid*."

"Kids have guns."

Henry massaged his temples with one hand. "Not where I'm from," he said.

## A BRUTAL DESIGN

I turned my attention back to the music, which was reaching a kind of crescendo of watery blips. The movement came together in a swirl of disparate currents, each comprised of unique electronic noises—statics, scratches, interferences. When it finished, Henry popped out the tape and flipped it over. Side B was more of the same, and kids didn't have guns in Lyon, France. Another place I'd never been. I resisted the urge to ask more questions about Lyon, reminding myself to stay reflective and quiet.

"So you came here to run away from guns," Henry said.

"That's not it at all," I said. I was about to defend myself but thought better of it. I didn't know Henry. I told him my reasons were personal. He raised his hands in a backing-off motion. We drove on in silence. I thought I detected a change in his posture.

By the time we reached Exit 500, the sun had mostly disappeared behind hills laden with tilting cypresses. The exit ramp seemed to curve infinitely. From above it would look like we were traveling on an ouroboros, these loops of pavement and yellow and white paint and metal barriers. The ramp spat us out onto a desolate road one notch above dirt, and we traveled down into a valley bordered on both sides by those gentle hills and their sentinel cypresses. Once the sun had set completely, Henry suggested we drive the rest of the way with the windows down. I didn't object. I was starved for fresh air.

And this air was fresh. A cool, rejuvenating breeze entered the car, washing out our effluences and replacing them with a fresh, woodsy, and vaguely salty smell. I stuck my head out of the window like a dog and gulped it in. Between the trains and the car, I hadn't had a real deep breath in close to twenty-four hours.

I was immediately refreshed. I took the opportunity to pass the gas I'd been holding in for the last five hours. I glanced at Henry to see if he'd noticed. He wrinkled his nose and I blushed deeply, turning my face to the window to avoid eye contact. He must have sensed my embarrassment, for he ejected the tape and put in a new one. *"Tous les garçons et les filles"* began to play, and Henry sang along with a surprisingly sweet alto in the French that was his native tongue.

After the song's conclusion, Henry said, "You won't hear French in Duma. Don't get used to it."

"Too bad. I've always loved the sound of it."

"The city discourages the use of any language other than English."

"And yours is excellent. It's hard to believe it's not your first language."

"I put a lot of work into it," he said proudly. "It's the result of years of training. My best attempt at a non-regional, international accent." He held out his palm as if to display the words coming out of his mouth. "Personally, I think I sound like one of those wise guys from the movies." He scrunched his face strangely, made a gun with his pointer and thumb.

"You do sound wise," I said.

"In Duma, we try to get rid of the differences between people," he said. "No divisions. No power imbalances."

It sounded too good to be true, of course, but it was mostly in line with what Uncle had written. Fairness. Equality. Worker protection.

I said, "That's obviously impossible, though, right?"

"It's aspirational. I admire it."

"In my country, any time we hear that rhetoric we know an autocrat isn't far behind."

"This is different."

"That's what the autocrats always say."

Henry smirked. "I don't blame you for feeling that way," he said. "I guess you'll just have to see for yourself."

I let his words hang in the air and turned my attention to the outdoors, rushing past in the darkness. Lone streetlamps cast jaundiced cones of light onto the road. Cypress trees still appeared now and then, muted in the moonless night. Between the lamps I could see purple clouds tacked to the sky.

At last, Henry took a sharp turn that curved dramatically downward, even deeper into the valley. When we leveled out, we made one final turn, and civilization came into view: an inconceivably large structure, as wide and tall as a stadium, made out of one seemingly seamless chunk of concrete which served as a podium for an even more startling shape. From the podium rose a concrete shaft, upon which flowered a tulip-like cube, twice as tall as wide, and covered with segmented glazed glass windows. Light poured out of those windows, illuminating the carpark in front, and the rectangular artificial lake beside it. As we drew closer, I could make out the silhouettes of dozens of people inside the head of the tulip, huddled close together, perhaps dancing or in conversation. The elongated reflections of light warbled on the surface of the lake.

We drove on. I could hear the faint sounds of brass, of jazz—real jazz, not Muzak—leaking from the glass tulip. I was drawn to it: the sounds of the music, the figures in the glass. The calm but brooding presence of the building, which was gravitational, which seemed to hum in my ears. My mind raced as I thought of secret passages and corridors, of a maze of concentric circles spinning out into infinity. The room inside had to be enormous. I wanted to know what was beneath the tulip, too, in the structure on which the flower stood.

"Listen," Henry said, as we drove into a new section of Duma. "What I said before, about where I'm from, just—just don't tell anyone about it, okay? I shouldn't have said anything. I regret it. It's between us. Okay?"

He had slowed the car down and was mostly looking at me now, suddenly rattled.

"Okay?" he said again. "Okay?"

"Fine, sure," I said. It hadn't occurred to me to catalog this detail for later use. In fact, I probably would have forgotten, if it weren't for his comment. Now I'd take pains not to.

I liked Henry, but you never know.

By the same token, I feared that I'd said something I shouldn't have, too. I definitely shouldn't have said the word *autocrat*.

19

"I won't tell anyone," I said.

He relaxed, and we sped up. I could make out the darkened shapes of more ordinary buildings now, large and small, fronted with glass and reinforced gray concrete. Long flat roofs with uninterrupted lines. I asked Henry where he was taking me. He said he was "under instruction" to drop me at the residency for new arrivals. He called it "The Crescent." He would personally show me to my room, he said, and in the morning, someone would call for me. I felt a wave of relief that I wouldn't have to report to someone tonight. Little floating neon fibers flashed in the periphery of my vision. I was exhausted.

"One more turn," said Henry.

We curved down a gravelly street that gave way to grass, then stopped abruptly at a glass-sided building that reflected our headlights back at us like two bulging yellow eyes as we pulled into a parking space. The building was boomerang-shaped, two or three stories tall, its many panes of glass staggered at uneven intervals with silver mullions in between—dividing the apartments, I gathered. It was a large enough curve that when I got out of the car, the length of it stretched past either side of me, leaving me in the dark inner part of the crescent. If every resident of the building looked out of their windows, they would all see me.

Henry appeared at my side with my bag. My one bag. Who knew what they had packed for me? Not my own clothes, surely. I shuddered to think who these new ones had belonged to before they wound up in my possession. I shuddered to think what it would feel like when I slipped into them. Would it feel like I was wearing someone else's skin? Would I forget myself?

The only possessions I had that were really mine were the money in my wallet, my jacket, and my keys to the house on Alizabet Street.

We walked along the building's curve until a door appeared, seamlessly, in the façade's continuous glass membrane. Lights came on one by one as I trailed Henry down the hall, doors on one side, clean, cool concrete on the other. As soon as the next motion-sensing light switched on, the one behind us shut off, so it was like walking slowly around the circle of a zoetrope, the lights illuminating each frozen step of our orbital journey. Every twenty yards or so we reached an opening in the ceiling that rose the full height of the building, terminating with a small glass dome through which I could make out stars. Henry halted after we passed under one of these. Our architecture at home was rudimentary, compared to this. I couldn't even name the materials used. "Here we are," he said. He took a key out of his jacket pocket and let us in.

The room was long but not wide, with everything laid out railroad-style. A living area fitted with cherry-red modular furniture sat against the glass wall, where blinds were drawn. There was a bare-bones kitchenette featuring a single-burner induction stove plugged into a wall outlet and a minifridge; a large print of abstract geometric shapes hanging on the wall opposite the kitchen; and a curtain at the far end of the room, beyond which, I presumed, I'd find a recess for a bed.

Henry nudged me out of the way and moved into the living area, where he put my bags down. Then he placed his hands on the small of his back and stretched so that his chin pointed up at the cast-cement waffle ceiling. When he finished, he stood there silently; I could make out points of light in his eyes. He surveyed me. Either he was about to attack me, or he was waiting for a tip. It was true: he had just driven me hundreds of miles and lugged my bags about like a chauffeur. I began to reach for my wallet. This seemed to do the trick, for Henry took a few paces toward me and stopped, expectantly, as I took out the wallet and started to unfold it. But before I could give him anything, he plucked it from my hands and quickly stored it in his back pocket. He smiled apologetically, though I did detect a hint of arrogance in his eyes.

"Doctor's orders," he said. I didn't have it in me to protest. He put a hand on my shoulder and squeezed, and told me: "You'll get a call in the morning. Get some rest. I'm sure I'll see you around. It's not so big here, anyway. Good night." He turned to leave but I caught him by the elbow.

"Wait," I whispered. "Do you drive people from the station often?"

Henry's eyes narrowed. "Why?"

"I'm looking for someone. My uncle."

"Hey, I don't know anything."

"Where were those other people being taken?"

"What people?"

"The people from the other compartments."

Henry drew close to me. "I drive the people who see their name on my signs," he said. "I don't drive anyone but them." He smiled at me—sadly, I thought—then left.

I plopped down on the plush red chaise lounge by the wall of windows and looked out across the living room. Now that I was finally alone, it felt like something hostile had just happened. I hadn't been expecting the welcome of a luxury hotel's concierge, but I *had* expected a welcome of some kind, and not just from Henry the driver. I thought at least there'd be a packet, a folder of informative documents, a campus map, a list of vital services. For instance: I was hungry. Where would I get food at this hour? At home, the meager foodstuffs I wrung out of my ration card hadn't produced nearly enough food to get me through twenty-four hours of traveling without my stomach eating itself.

I roused myself from the chair and rummaged in the kitchen. I couldn't bring myself to find the light switch, and anyway my eyes had adjusted to the darkness. I found the handle on the minifridge—a horizontal metal handle; even the fridge was stylized, Streamline Moderne—and clicked it open, knowing full well it'd be empty.

The light blasted me, froze me. I saw stars. Then I saw food products. A dazzling array of products in perfect geometric order: rectangular cartons of water and milk and juice, white with bold black sans-serif lettering; a square metal container containing apples and oranges and grapes, their colors practically vibrating; nutrition bars in crisp clean plastic; condiments in identical tubes

# A BRUTAL DESIGN

stacked side by side in the fridge door panel; a loaf of bread in crinkle wrapper; a crisper drawer full of lettuce, onion, pepper, and garlic; and several vacuum-sealed packages of synthetic meat. I stood before the glowing minifridge and stuffed myself with fruit, then washed it down with juice. It had probably been years since I'd eaten that much produce. When I finished, I closed the fridge, plunging the room back into darkness. I found the wall and followed it. When I felt the curtain, I pushed through, and fell onto a bed on the other side.

# TWO

**W**HEN I WOKE UP, the curtain was a heap of metal and fabric at the edge of the bed. I must have pulled the rod down in the night. Morning light filtered in from the living room. The heat was stifling. I hadn't undressed; my shoes were still on. The clock on the nightstand read eight-thirty. I rolled onto my back and something crinkled beneath me. A glossy, candy-red file folder, stamped with a crest that looked like a modernist variant of the caduceus: a central rod entwined with angular cables, which flowed into—a satellite dish? It looked more like a cobra's hood. Curving lines—radio waves—emanated from the shape. Inside the folder was a campus map, along with a short note on heavy-stock stationary:

S— Zelnik: We are pleasing to welcome you to Duma. If you would to join us for orientations and refreshments in Fulcrum at 1000. We will acquaint with you and inquire about your questions.

—Management

I examined the map. It wasn't hard to locate the Crescent, central as it was and so absurdly shaped. But the rest of the map was difficult to read. The location names were mostly blurred beyond legibility, though I was able to get a sense of a central district where most things were clustered. The fact that the surrounding area had been redacted made it seem as if the desert were eating through Duma's periphery, a menacing encroachment that would eventually swallow the settlement whole. It was more likely that there were elements in the areas beyond that Duma wanted kept secret. I was no stranger to maps with redactions. Where I came from, it was impossible to get an accurate city map. Avenues were never where the maps said they'd be; buildings seemed to shift a block north, a block south, depending on which map you were looking at. Addresses changed over time like rock formations licked by erosion. A so-called security measure, we supposed, a way of keeping detailed descriptions out of the hands of "the enemy." But our only enemies were our leaders. Redacting the maps only piled more attention onto the hidden objects anyway.

I looked at the map carefully, trying to discern where I could go to ask about my uncle. Maybe a registrar, or a clerk's office if there was one. The fact that I didn't know exactly when he'd arrived would probably make it more complicated. By the map, Duma looked pretty big, I could imagine dozens if not hundreds of new people arriving daily. In any case, orientation in an hour meant that he'd have to wait anyway. He could stand to wait. And I would have to be fine with letting him wait. I wondered if they'd told him I was coming.

I undressed, found the bathroom—windowless, ventless, a metal showerhead placed on the wall above a lidless toilet so that I had to lean fully over the toilet bowl when I showered—and rinsed, shaved, freshened. I couldn't remember what the weather had been like when we arrived. I felt the adrenaline of displacement as I dressed in the best-fitting clothes I could find in my bag: slacks a size too tight, a purple button-down with flared cuffs, and, of course, my pride, what I'd been wearing for the last twenty-four hours, the only meaningful artifact in my possession: a tan corduroy sport coat which had been my uncle's. He'd bequeathed it to me one day after I complimented him on it. He took it off then and there and thrust it at me, telling me I'd get it now or soon enough, so it might as well be now. Ordinarily, this would be the kind of mawkishness I would resent—why did he always believe the torments of his inner life would find footholds among the torments of mine, would supplant them?—but I loved that jacket dearly. I felt it looked better on me than it ever could have looked on him and his nearly fleshless bones. I pictured his face when he saw me wearing it and smiled to myself, admitting to a bit of schadenfreude. I ate one nutrition bar, pocketed another, and left my room, map in hand.

It took a minute or so to get outside; I became suspicious that I was going the wrong way down the curving hallway, turned, and went back. It was ten to nine when I found the exit, pushed the glass door wide, and realized that it hadn't mattered which way I walked from my apartment since there were exits at both ends of the Crescent leading to the same place. I stepped into the sandy valley and into the sun, which had crested the cypress trees on the ridges. In front of me was the grassy carpark and a heap of recently emptied garbage bins, all sporting the same crest as the red folder. Several raised garden beds stood off by the foot of the hill, crowded with juvenile vegetation.

I wandered a bit, looking for the main road that would lead me to the Fulcrum building. I crossed a courtyard, smelling kerosene, hearing the hum of a faraway engine. The nearby buildings were in the brutalist style, imposing and utilitarian, a contrast to the cool but cheap glass architecture of the Crescent. Beyond them sandy paths arced over hills that were barren except for cypresses.

There were other people around, many of them wearing denim overalls and white shirts, or austere jumpsuits laden with pockets. They held toolboxes or briefcases, walked in pairs or alone, and appeared to run the spectrum of age from twenty to fifty, though one man did cross my path with a spine so bent he couldn't have been younger than seventy. Some of the people nodded at me, or even smiled. There was no common denominator among them that I could perceive. No dominant skin tone, no gender more prevalent than another. Snippets of language floated through the hot air. All of it accented English. I had to stop so a pair of girls in pleated skirts could skip past holding hands. They laughed their way across a hosed-down courtyard where little pools of water flickered in the dusty sunshine.

There was something about the diversity that I found perturbing. I wasn't used to it. Instead of feeling like the hallmark of a progressive, multicultural society—people from all over the world meeting in grassy fields, shaking hands, smiling in the sun—it made Duma feel like a transit camp.

I walked another quarter mile before consulting the map, turning it twice before we understood each other. It told me to take Reeps Street, which I did, walking alongside two parallel, overgrown ditches probably meant for trolley tracks. The Fulcrum building appeared: a thundering concrete shed that rose five stories above a bustling courtyard filled with bench-like concrete slabs and concrete planters filled with spiky desert plants. People milled about with their briefcases and backpacks, wearing more work uniforms—overalls and hardhats; suits and assorted office attire. Some sat on the concrete slabs, eating apples and reading newspapers. The Fulcrum building loomed over them, blotting out the sun and blanketing the courtyard in shade. It lacked any real architectural detail: just a malformed block of material with thin, vertical glass windows stenciled into the concrete, and only one larger concentration of glass: a meeting space that cantilevered over the courtyard in the shape of the letter *T*. In the sunshine beyond the shadowy courtyard, there was mud.

The lobby was a windowless, intimidating tunnel, its sloping walls creating the illusion that it was swallowing itself. A man in a black suit stood behind a concrete block, illuminated by a mushroom-shaped brass lamp bright enough to make me squint. He looked like he could have been from anywhere—an unplaceable skin tone, Jordanian, maybe, or Dutch, or Siberian. He wore his hair in a ponytail as black as his suit. It was still wet from the shower and pulled back so tightly that not a single hair was free. I had never met anyone this serious who had a ponytail.

I showed him the note I'd received from "Management." He glanced at it briefly.

"There's an elevator behind me," he said. "You're on the fourth floor." Then he fed the note through a shredder behind the concrete slab and handed me a name tag. "Pin it on your breast." It was gold-colored with my name scrawled in black marker.

The elevator released me onto a cavernous floor with the same cast-cement waffle ceiling as my apartment, only several stories up. Doors lined the walls. Another desk, another concrete block, another concierge tracking my approach—this time a woman with soft features, a broad forehead, and bobbed red hair. She wore dark brown lipstick and smiled when I said hello. My voice echoed off the walls. She consulted my name tag, then consulted a folder on the block before her.

"Room 2B," she said. She leaned over the block and pointed to a door behind me, a little to the left. "Just over there," she said, her suit fabric crinkling. Her breath smelled fresh with peppermint.

My heels clicked loudly against the Grand Antique

marble floor. A room furnished like this, with a floor like this—I couldn't imagine the expense, the effort required to haul the materials out into the middle of the desert. A plaque on the door read *Processing*. I entered and met a bank of chairs arranged against a concrete wall. They faced another cement block, with another concierge behind it. This one gestured kindly to an empty chair halfway down the wall. The rest of the chairs were occupied by men and women. Some sat forward, their elbows resting on their knees; others reclined with folded legs. We all looked very different from each other. No one spoke; no music played. They stared into space or rested with their eyes closed. I wondered if they were new arrivals like me. Or perhaps they were here to be repurposed, like how Henry had gone from dentistry to chauffeuring. Some of them seemed nervous, but I might have been projecting. *I* was nervous. Imposing, anonymous architecture, vast windowless interiors, echoing hallways. This was egalitarianism in building form, yet I did not feel reassured. Back home, a building meant for the processing of people into classes of varying importance would reveal its purpose through pompous Neoclassical flourishes and stately columns. Architecture that did everything it could to tell you that you were not worthy. This was the opposite, yet deep within me the worry wouldn't settle. Where I came from, you did not transition from a waiting room into greener pastures.

A clock ticked on the wall. We waited. One by one, fifteen minutes apart, my neighbors were called through a closed door at the end of a hallway. It was hot in the room, poorly ventilated. I grew sleepy, still jet-lagged, many time zones behind.

I worried that waiting would be my only activity here. I worried that I had made a catastrophic error in following Uncle here, in taking the bait, in not putting up a scrappier fight. For all its own horrors, I worried that I would never see home again, or Mela and Elam, or my university, which resented my membership, or my drafty house, which attracted pranksters, or my streets, which were filled with the rotting bodies of dogs. And I worried that my name would never be called.

My name was called.

I shook my head free of the heat and stood. The concierge gestured to the hallway behind her and entered through the unmarked door into a terribly long room with a low, claustrophobic ceiling, inlaid with vents and lights.

There was a sculpture at the far end of the room, oriented away from me so that I was looking at its rear. It was a fish, I guessed—I identified something like a tailfin. The body was attached to metal stands that were attached to a concrete podium. I squinted to understand it better but couldn't. As I was looking, someone cleared their throat. A woman was standing by the door, middle-aged, with brunette hair that fell in ringlets over her collarbone. She wore blocky red glasses and a form-fitting jumpsuit. A small person who stood so erect that I felt I was in for a time-out.

"Do you like sharks?"

The question startled me. "I don't know."

"You must know," she said gamely. She closed the gap between us. A band of freckles peppered the bridge of her nose.

"I never thought about it before. Sure. I like them."

"This is a basking shark." She extended her hand like a tour guide and began to walk. I caught up and followed. Her accent was unplaceable. I thought about Henry's accent-reduction training as I listened to the unnatural cadences in her speech, its alien timbre. I thought about why English was Duma's lingua franca and what that said about the people that made up its governing body, whether they thought of English as a superior language— or a more strategically useful one. Then I realized that I hadn't been paying attention.

"They're filter feeders," she was explaining, "meaning they filter out the inessential. Scientists call them a cosmopolitan migratory species because they go wherever there are temperate oceans. They swim slowly along, water passing through them." She made wave motions with her hand. "Gill rakers, little bonelike bits of cartilage, capture traveling plankton. The basking shark is the second-largest extant shark, the only surviving member of the family *Cetorhinidae*."

She stopped suddenly. I could now see most of the shark's profile. It looked real enough to be an actual specimen. Its skin was mottled, a kind of sickly brown-gray pattern. A patina of striated stains and shapes ran along its body. If it was a replica, then it was a truly outstanding one. There was a caudal fin, huge and sail-like, a dorsal fin, and two separate fins on each side, one much larger than the other. I didn't know what those fins were called. Gallery lights shone onto the shark, illuminating it in three separate cones.

"You understand that the shark is a metaphor, yes?"

I liked to think in terms of metaphor. I was studying to be an architect. I believed first and foremost in representation. I believed that every built thing casts a shadow; that the shadows say as much if not more than the structure; that structure both is defined by and defines builder and dweller; that all homes are also the signs of homes; that all buildings are symbolic of buildings; and that all constructs of whatever kind are signs and symbols.

I had no idea what the shark stood for.

"Of course," I said.

"Tell me of what."

The woman watched me watching the shark. Aware of this, my heartbeat began to race. It occurred to me that I was being tested. She might be a psychologist of some kind, evaluating my reactions to our conversation. The shark was a Rorschach Test, an ink blot, my reaction to it determining my worth, my aptitude, my function—was I inspired by it? Afraid of it? Did I empathize with its plight, how tragic it was to have been made a tool of cognitive appraisal rather than remaining free to bask and filter and be a member of a cosmopolitan migratory species?

I felt the coldness of the room and shivered involuntarily. I looked at the woman: she wore a vacant smile with the practiced ease of a doctor delivering bad news. Despite the cold, I realized I was sweating. My jaw began to hurt. To my great relief, she turned away and resumed walking, this time in silence, until she was close enough to the sculpture to run her hand along its body.

"I came here because Duma represented a cohesion between labor and human worth that, in my country, was seen as outlandish," she began. "A place where workers could find fulfilment in their work, where they could be treated with humanity. To work for the benefit of a common goal and see the rewards of their labor. Yes, this is why I came here. Because I *had* to come here, do you see? In my country, we were worked until we had no life left. Forced collectivization left our farms decimated and our people to die. My mother and father watched soldiers load *our* tractors and *our* carriages with *our* wheat and drive them away into the city, to feed people who would become other soldiers, soldiers who would return to the countryside to repeat the ugly process in a cycle that Nietzsche predicted as the eternal return. Nevertheless, my mother and father decided to stay on their so-called farm, to die of starvation or be raped to death. I ran away. I left my family behind; they did not understand. I came to where I would be valued. Where I could see workers love their work; where the peasantry ate the food they grew, or gave it to a greater good that *they* believed in. Where the things I made with my hands would join other handmade objects and sculptures far larger than this building, far more valuable than you or I."

She gazed at the shark admiringly.

"What happened to your family?" I asked.

She turned fiercely to me and said, "No one has family in Duma."

I decided I would not ask this woman to help me find my uncle.

"There were people in my country that were valued more than other people in my country," she said. "The people with more value were able to consolidate the power. They had control over everything. Even the way you think."

I recognized elements from my country, too, in her tale of corruption. I thought, maybe, that I could find like-minded people here—people who could help me. I suddenly understood the metaphor.

"Does the shark represent Duma?" I said. "The shark filters out the malignancies in the ideology. The cancer that breeds corruption."

"It purifies the water," said the woman. She seemed proud of me. Against my better judgment, I felt proud of me, too.

She threaded her arm through mine and escorted me to the front of the shark, but I watched her. I congratulated myself on getting on her good side. Fans in the ceiling whirred to life. Cool, musty air blew on my neck. Old air.

"What will you do?" she asked.

"With what?"

She tilted her head toward the shark and, at last, giving into the temptation I had strangely been resisting, I looked. I stepped back in horror. It was an appalling face, with the snout of a manatee and the mouth of the devil. I didn't see its eyes in the two globular bulges above; I didn't see anything but the dark. The universe collapsed into its mouth. A bucket of ringed bones, the gill arches, looped around the cavern of the mouth cavity, spaced every few inches, and hundreds, thousands, of tiny hooked teeth sprouted like grass. My vision blurred. I reached out in space and found the woman's elbow. She shook free of my hand and stepped away.

"Go ahead," she said. "Put your head in it."

"What?" I tried to find her face but couldn't see well enough. The room began to tilt. Everything was askew.

"Do it," she said. "You must do it."

"I don't even know your name," I said, dumbfounded.

"What difference does it make?" She had become openly hostile. Her smile was gone, her tone defiant.

"Is this part of the test?" I careened forward and grabbed onto the snout of the shark, my head hanging limply between my shoulders.

"When will I receive my grade?" I asked. It wasn't what I'd meant to say.

"That's up to you," she said. I twisted my head to see an inversion of her. She glanced at her watch, then at the ceiling, then back at me. "Well?"

I turned back to the basking shark and its seductive mouth. I saw through its throat into the vertigo of abyss. The path at the end of the abyss rushed forward as I fell backwards, but I fell backwards into the mouth. My head entered the horizon of the mouth and above and below and on all sides of me were rows and rows of crooked baby teeth, bending in toward me as I fell further inside. My vision blurred again, and then was gone. Before my head hit the bent scaffolding of the gill arches, I had a thought that I was doing the right thing. That I was on the right path. I was confident that I had made the correct choice. Inside of me an oven of ecstasy fired to life.

I woke in a stuffy half-light, feeling a headache blooming where they usually do in the nook between my right eye and eyebrow. I massaged the nook with my thumb. I felt hungover, sensitive to the light, but I couldn't remember drinking. I was sure I hadn't: drinking for me came with a paroxysmal stomach, nausea. I didn't have those—I only had the headache.

I rolled onto my side and noticed a folder on the nightstand. I must have brought it back with me after my meeting in the Fulcrum, though I was struggling to remember what had happened once I'd left the building. I was aware of a sense of uncertainty, of displacement in my mind as I thought about it. And then I realized: I couldn't account for the time. I sat up, horrified—tried to focus on remembering, but it wasn't there. It wasn't coming to me. I was overwhelmed with feelings of self-hatred and disgust, as if I had done something humiliating, something unforgivable. What was it?

It was late morning, past ten. I rubbed my eyes, then opened the folder across my lap. There was a note inside.

S— Zelnik: Congratulations to you and welcome to you to Duma. It is your pleasure to be assigned to Factory 7A. We have reviewed the data information you have provided to us with and determined that your field of labor will be:

## MANUAL LABOR

We are pleasing to invite you to arrive at Factory 7A tomorrow at 0800. Please to take this day to acquaint yourself with Duma. You may take a bus from Beau Gino Plaza. Please to address concerns to foreman at site of work.

Manual labor? Clearly a bureaucratic error. They didn't need me for manual labor. *Nobody* needed me for manual labor. Flat feet, bad knees, a snake of a spine— misaligned, weak, short of vertebrae. Blocked sinuses, spiritual malaise, itchy eyes. There was no reason to have undertaken the great expense of sending me out here only to assign me to a manual labor outfit. My training would be wasted. Besides, there were undoubtedly hundreds of thousands of people in reasonable geographical proximity to Duma who would be more than grateful for the opportunity to work. This place was an Eden compared to most communities that dotted the globe. People would sell their families out for a chance to sleep in a bed as soft as this one. For a chance to be assigned a job, to earn a wage. Simply having a job was a privilege for much of the world.

Not that there was anything wrong with manual labor. The world was built on the bent and flagellated backs of workers, and I was proud to have once associated with a movement that championed their rights, even if we had to do so secretly, namelessly, through the dissemination of subversive material on utility poles in plazas.

Nevertheless, the idea of engaging in it embarrassed me.

I wouldn't take no for an answer. I knew that it would be wiser to keep my head down and accept the position I'd been assigned, but I believed too much in my craft to be complacent. And I wanted to believe in the promise of Duma. I wanted to believe that there were better, kinder places out there—out *here*—in the world. The note said I could address my concerns to the foreman at the factory. I would do just that. That's what I would do.

It was time to get up. I got out of bed and made it, dressed and washed, then fished through the minifridge and made a sandwich out of two chunks of gooey wheat bread and several slices of the vacuum-sealed synthetic meat, which was rubbery and salty and tasted vaguely like bologna and cheddar. I wiped the crumbs and ran the tap, which spread a sulfuric odor through the room. A laminated note above the sink assured me that the water was safe to drink despite the smell. As I choked it down, I wondered when I'd hear from Uncle—or if he'd even learned yet that I'd made it.

When I locked up, I noticed a note had been tacked to the door. *Come by the cluster of houses on the hill and say hi.* Well, there was my answer: he had found me already. I took a deep breath and consulted the map. There were shapes that somewhat resembled a cluster of houses a bit south of the Crescent.

It was already hot; my sweat already saturated the

liner of the coat. Worried that I'd soak through the map, I refolded it and tucked it into an outer pocket. Uncle would be surprised to see the jacket even if he wasn't surprised to see me. Truthfully, I had no idea how he would react to seeing me. His letter hadn't been an invitation, exactly. Half manifesto of excuses masquerading as bridge-building, half wildly unintelligible zealotry about Duma. It had been over a year since I'd last seen or heard from him, until that letter arrived. He hadn't left us a forwarding address when he went away, only a terse goodbye note, making it clear that his intention was to sever his relationships. The truth is we had figured him for dead, figured he had left this cruel world at last, taking one last stab at being the driving force in his own life by choosing to end it.

I wish I could say that my reaction to hearing the news that not only was he alive but that he'd been sent here as a chemical engineer to do something useful was one of pleasant surprise—but it wasn't. Mostly I just felt dread and irritation. You had a full year to send a letter home to Alizabet Street, to let Mela and Elam know you were all right, to let *me* know you were all right—and you didn't. It didn't even cross your mind, I'd bet. It was a fantasy that you'd worried about us, about me. And now, a fantasy that you would care that I was here in Duma. In the years before you left, the years after your return from the *first* time you were imprisoned, you stopped worrying about your own personal hygiene, failing to bathe for days on end. And you certainly didn't care about the lives of others, even those closest to you, the ones who took care of you—who reminded you to bathe. So why would you care that I was here now?

But to not even let Mela or Elam know—that was selfish. Unspeakable. They took care of you for years, more than I ever did—more than you ever let me. You owed it to them to let them know. They would have seen the letter when they collected your mail every week, as they had for the last year, *just in case*. They didn't know worrying about you was a one-way street. I'd tell them myself. They were too good to you. Your suffering never made you virtuous.

I hadn't been paying attention to where I was walking, lost in the fantasy argument I would have with Uncle when I saw him. When I took in what was around me, I found that I was standing at the boundary of a cluster of short, modular homes sitting on a hill, small enough to be single-family homes but big enough to be impressive. They had small, decorative perimeter walls that were raised and lowered and broken and fragmented as the builder had seen fit and etched with geometric patterns. Beautiful, functionless walls.

# THREE

THE HOUSES BEHIND THE WALLS were beautiful too, with front rooms shaped like shipping containers jutting out over small, grassy yards. They had flat roofs and smooth concrete walls with wide rectangular windows or thin vertical slits. Some of the houses lacked traditional corners—where the concrete walls met, they met at glass. Vertical glass panes set into the concrete in place of corners, so that the walls never touched. The houses seemed impressionable, mutable, while being utterly permanent. The glass made me think that if I lived in one of these houses, I could enter or leave through any wall—that nothing was bound, that there were infinite paths through the space.

I realized that I was looking at the first evidence I'd seen of Duma's progressive architectural bona fides. These were malleable, changeable constructions. Built for additions and annexes, for easy and affordable expansions and contractions. They were utilitarian but had personalized flair. I admired them and was hungry to work on something similar.

But I wondered how you wound up in one of these houses. Why had I been assigned a room in the Crescent? There were individual gardens attached to the houses, gardens in full flourish. The real farms must have been elsewhere in Duma, maybe in the borderlands. Too many people needed to be fed to grow everything in personal gardens. These were luxury gardens. For hobby, for fun. Imagine working the land for entertainment. Imagine growing produce for the novelty of it. Sparing a tenth of your land for flowers.

Inequality sowed discord. Case in point: I was jealous. I heard a metallic-sounding thunk and followed it to find a man working in his personal garden, on his knees in his own soil, in his own backyard, stabbing at the ground with a long metal hoe—for fun. He wore khaki work pants and muddy white shirtsleeves and gripped the hoe with gardening gloves. He worked diligently, bringing the hoe above his bald head and swinging it down powerfully, piercing the dirt with a satisfying clunk. His lips pulled back into a grimace, flaring not from exertion, I didn't think, but from concentration, from thinking he was alone. His lips tautened and relaxed like that again and again in a kind of tic. There was no one else around; the sun had passed its zenith but was just as intense. Impressive toiling in this heat. Watching him made me feel like I was getting away with something. He knelt in a row of mostly upturned soil. Green on either side of him: tomato plants snaking up trellises, carrots, kale, Swiss chard, vegetables I didn't recognize.

Eventually he rose to his feet and peeled his gloves off, wiping the sweat from his forehead with the inside of his forearm. And then he turned, and we made eye contact. There was a long pause in which we took each other in: his build was sturdy, but he stooped, which made him look meek, like someone easily taken advantage of. He had open, kind eyes and a hairless face. I wanted to know what his assessment of me was. We only really think of ourselves when we look another in the eyes.

He waved and called hello. I walked up the short hill to his wall, reaching into my jacket pocket for a handkerchief. My hands were slick with sweat and I didn't want to disgust him. I smiled politely at him as I withdrew, instead, the map, which was now soaked through with sweat despite my efforts. The black ink was smudged and illegible.

"Uh oh," he said, looking at the soggy paper. "That's not good." He put his hand out. I wiped my palms on my trousers and we shook. He had a sporting handshake.

"I get sweaty," I said. This was a disappointing thing to say. He had crosshatching beneath his eyes, like the skin had been flayed. I looked at his garden instead. "Nice garden," I said. I introduced myself, though my attention was elsewhere. I scanned the area for Uncle.

Hearing my name, he gave me an odd look. "Thanks," he said. "Erich Snelling." He rubbed the back of his neck bashfully and glanced at the garden. "Just a pet project of mine. Of all of ours, really."

I didn't want to be rude by running off too quickly. I'd chat him up for a while, then move on. "So what happens, you grow food and then contribute to a community program, or what?"

"No, I eat the food I grow. But there are competitions. It's good fun." He gestured to his neighbors' gardens, each perfectly manicured into rows of bursting greenery. "The broccoli, in particular. It's—ah." He fell into reverie.

"How did you wind up here instead of in the—"

"The Crescent," he said, smiling knowingly. "I'm sorry it took so long for us to meet."

"I only arrived yesterday."

With an expression halfway between a smile and a grimace, Erich offered a hearty, "Well then, welcome!" His teeth were small but straight and gleaming; they put an image to the phrase *pearly whites*. "I'm glad you found me. I realized after I left it how vague my note was."

There was a pang in my stomach. "You wrote the note?"

He gave a small bow. "Who else?"

The pang persisted, and I realized that it wasn't only disappointment but also gastrointestinal distress. A splinter of pain lodged itself in the right side of my abdomen. I shoved my hands in my pockets and pressed my fingernails into my thighs through the fabric, digging for distraction. I thought about my breakfast of synthetic meats. The pockmarked, pale red surface of the meat, the way the individual slices congealed into a brick, how thin, clingy strings of mucus stretched between them when I spun for a moment then

e had joined the "move-
, when Duma was just four
ozen settlers. When the first
ose one and moved in. It was
philosophy of communal housing
end to the construction of individual
shifted to buildings like the Crescent.
in the naming," he said.
o me that he'd know Henry. "He picked
he station."

scratched his head. "Sorry. No bells."
did want to clarify one thing about the gardens,
gh. "They're not just for pleasure," he said. "The
na Agricultural Agency is constantly churning out
xperimental land-use products. New fertilizers, crop supplements, et cetera. We test the products for them and gather data. This," he said, peeling a prehistorically giant fan of kale from a stalk, "is the result of an advanced fertilizer that's had some success. Never mind that it's a red Russian varietal."

"Is that a—bad kale?" I asked. "I don't know kales."
"It's Russian," said Erich. "The state doesn't get along well with the Russians."
"Not surprising."
Erich released the leaf and it sprung back to the stalk.
"Do you need a drink or something?"
"Why?"
"No offense, but you look terrible."

The spin-
t a little
trouble
side.
ing
n I

"I guess I don't feel well," I conceded. [...]ning hadn't come back, but the nausea had. I fe[...] feverish, but mostly I felt uncertain. I was having [...] remembering where I was.

"Stay right there," said Erich. "Don't move."

He left me to sway in the garden while he went in[...] After what felt like a very long time, he emerged hold[...] a glass of water. He handed it to me, but I recoiled whe[...] brought it to my lips. That same noxious eggy odor.

"It's just the sulfur. You'll get used to it. Drink up."

I closed my eyes and gulped it down. It threatened to come back up, then settled uneasily in my stomach.

Erich led me to one of the lower garden walls and sat me down. I looked up at him—his bald pate silhou-etted by the sun—and realized that he looked familiar to me. But I didn't know if it was recognition from only moments earlier, or if I'd known him sometime in the past. His accent was like mine, or similar enough. His tongue seemed to snag on the diphthongs, dragging them under.

"Anyway," he said. "Duma is territory with infra-structure, law, taxes. The idealism is real, the goals are concrete, the people are happy. It's completely different from where we came from. In all the best ways. It seems like there's less. But there is much, much more. We have a welfare system, for Christ's sake."

This time when he smiled, I saw that one of his front teeth was dead and gray and leaned like an old headstone to the right, and I realized that it wasn't déjà vu I was experiencing but genuine recognition.

"How do you know where I'm from? I asked.

Erich laughed, but when I didn't laugh with him, he tilted his head. "We're not just doing this for...?" His lips pulled into that hostile smile.

I didn't respond. How did I know him?

"This is too funny," he said. "I thought we were doing a bit. You don't remember me, do you?"

"I'm sorry. I can't place you."

"We were at Barnova together. Erich Snelling. It doesn't ring a bell?" He ran his hand over his head sheepishly. "People called me Eddy. I used to get mad when they called me Eddy. I couldn't get rid of it. We were in Hallen's class together. You remember. Eddy. Erich. Eddy."

I recognized him in a violent flash, a younger version of him, a horrible image of him from that period seared onto my mind. I knew him well.

I needed to leave.

"I didn't know your name was Erich." I started to angle away but he got in front of me again.

"That's me."

"I'm sorry if I ever called you Eddy."

"Don't worry about it. I got over it. Don't have the anger stuff anymore. I'm not that person anymore. I genuinely thought you were doing a bit just now. People reinvent themselves here all the time. You probably know about the accent thing?"

I nodded, afraid of him.

"I thought that's what you were doing, pretending not to remember me. Do what you want, you know? Duma is a city of tabulae rasae. No one knows what anyone did before they showed up here. It's the beauty of the place. God, it's been, what, six, seven years?"

"Something like that."

We shared a painful silence in which I tried to figure out how to excuse myself. He seemed lost in thought.

"Oh, you'll like this," he said suddenly, as if in answer to a question. "You know Miriana Grannoff? The artist? She's here, too. Came to Duma a few years ago. She's been beautifying the place. Making it cosmopolitan. Worldly. You'll see her work sooner or later."

This, too, shocked me. To say that I admired Grannoff's work would be an understatement. I was religious about it. But more importantly, her presence in Duma was the best endorsement of this place I could ever hope to get, given that she was famously a leftist artist, known for uncanny, lifelike fabrications that she often employed in activist contexts as statements against war, famine, disease, corruption. Like some of my favorite professors, Grannoff had been a casualty of the purge of Barnova's left-leaning faculty members and had, we'd thought, emigrated to South America. Thinking about Grannoff being here made me relax a bit, but then I remembered who I was talking to.

"I took a class with her," I said.

"You're lucky. I didn't know who she was. Otherwise, I would have taken one, too." He glanced over his shoulder at his house and I followed his gaze. A shadow passed by the window inside. "Listen," he said. "The garden isn't going to hoe itself. It was good to see you again."

I swallowed the urge to turn and run. "Erich, I'm looking for someone," I said. "Is there an address book, a directory—something like that?"

He raised his eyebrows. "Who are you looking for? Maybe I know her. We all know each other."

"My uncle. His name—"

"Uncle Zelnik!"

"You know him? Could you tell me where he is?"

"Sorry, no. I don't know him. But any uncle of yours is an uncle of mine. I'll let you know if I see him."

We shook hands and Erich embraced me, pulling me into the grotto of his body, essence of sweat and soil. When I tried to disengage, he pulled me even closer, near enough that his lips brushed my ear.

"You can do whatever you want here," he whispered. Then he turned back to tending his garden.

I picked a direction at random and headed away from the residential knolls, trying to remember what I could about Erich—Eddy, as he'd been called at Barnova. A withdrawn, awkward, occasionally antagonistic kid who took copious notes and hummed to himself while Professor Hallen lectured.

Hallen taught a course called Fascist Literature. The course catalogue offered it as an elective to satisfy the "Inflammatory Text Analysis" prerequisite, a requirement for all students at Barnova—a holdover from the university's founding a few lifetimes earlier. The idea had been to train college students to mine texts for right-wing incitement—intentional or incidental. Then, society could make progress toward eliminating the power of text as violence.

When I was a freshman, this philosophy was alive and well. Barnova was the kind of campus that released a fresh crop of activist intellectuals into the world with each commencement. It had been the alma mater of my loyal socialist parents. But by the time I was a junior, a new President had been elected, followed by a new Provost, a new Dean of Curriculum, and a new Dean of Students— all lackeys, it was rumored, of city officials.

Barnova's more progressive departments were defunded. Fortunately for me, the architecture program went untouched, but the humanities were scraped of aging professors and their replacements had dubious credentials. It left a bitter taste in our mouths that Hallen, who had been teaching this class for twenty years, had emerged unscathed from the restructuring. This evidence pointed toward a disingenuous liberalism on his part. His class was supposed to study hateful ideologies the same way epidemiologists study diseases: to understand and to cure. Instead, we juniors began to suspect, Hallen's class was designed less to prevent hate than to improve upon it. So I found myself in a class that ordinarily would have been filled with progressives but was now populated equally by right-wingers no longer afraid of daylight. I felt very uncomfortable in that class.

After I'd been wandering a while, I found a slab in the shade and took out my soggy map, unfolding it to assess the damage. It wasn't so illegible that I couldn't make out

Beau Gino Plaza, the city center, but using a few visible landmarks around me—an L-shaped office building, a children's swing set in a circle of depressed land—I was able to position myself. I let the map dry on the concrete for a while and then headed out again. I wanted to find a town hall, a public directory, a post office—anything that might have a list of residents, or a way to contact my uncle. It looked like I wanted to go east, so I followed a boulevard of cypresses that went on much farther than the map indicated it would and found myself lost again. My jacket was soaked through, turning its pinkish beige coloring an unattractive russet.

In Hallen's class, Erich's politics should have been clear enough from the outset. I recalled that there were outbursts. I remembered him erupting if there was too much of a kumbaya among the leftists as we read and dissected the writings of Hitler, Mussolini, and Mosley; the ideologies and texts of the American Tea Party or the Wang Jingwei regime. In earlier times, Professor Hallen _d have guided students toward seeing the fallacious _e unscientific claims and baseless accusations. _time I took the class, he mostly just let the _at each other. He seemed at times para- _tion, at times obsequious or simply indo-

_ought about it, the less sure I was of _I did know that Erich used to wear _—white painter pants, white polyes- _stic boots—and snap at anyone who _d people most certainly glanced at

Erich. His dark hair hung over his eyes; he took notes by wrapping his right arm entirely around the desk like an embankment meant to keep waves from crashing over. He was an angry kid. I remembered that occasionally, after a blowup, he'd be embarrassed, say that he was "only playing devil's advocate." Hallen encouraged this "free-spirited" debate. A little free-spirited debate never hurt anyone.

Erich's defenses were crass and unnuanced—they hunkered in logical pits he couldn't claw out of, so he spent his energy uselessly hurling himself at the crumbling walls. There were any number of other students in the class eager to show Eddy precisely how and why he was wrong, that his arguments about eugenics and racial purity or media control or economic manipulation were rooted in medieval thinking. But Barnova was expelling students for less. There were reasons to believe that informants posing as students were present in every class.

*That* Eddy was nothing like *this* Erich. I turned onto a wide dirt road that ran between long and low concrete buildings outfitted with glass curtain walls. What had happened to him? Where had that mad kid gone? Antagonism like his didn't just disappear so easily.

The buildings hulked over the road. Most were two or three stories, some with porticos shaded by brise soleil that projected gridded shadows onto the walkwa[...] Some were of plain reinforced gray concrete with[...] roofs. Others featured elegant explosions of geo[...] blocky and angular, octagonal, trapezoidal, hex[...] Grounded spaceships from modernist alien

Organized with thoughts of the sun. Complicated, comforting monuments to logic and rationalism, built to honor the people who dwelled within them, built with them in mind.

The ground I walked on was unpaved. A dry wind sprayed pebbles and dirt into my eyes. As I approached the city center, I noticed the lack of shopfronts. Most of the buildings seemed to begin at the second story, their ground floors devoted to exposed concrete supports and columns or airways that you could pass under if you wanted to get from this expanse of dirt to the one on the other side. It looked a bit like what I imagined the American Wild West must have looked like: wide, dusty streets pocked with divots and holes. I felt lightheaded and sat down on some more misshapen concrete. It seemed like I couldn't walk more than half a mile without getting exhausted. Where was my energy? I closed my eyes and felt the ground shifting beneath my feet, but the sensation passed after a minute or two. I looked both ways down the lane through air that quivered in the heat. A sharp pain rang through my head and for a moment I forgot what I was doing here. I got up slowly and checked the map, oriented myself as best as I could, and set out.

I reached Beau Gino Plaza abruptly. A wide and shaded square, bordered by the usual cypresses but also by swaying palm trees. Here, there were shopfronts. Advertisements, too. On posterboard, tacked to the few telephone poles or to freestanding advertising structures. Reminders to enroll children in the free nursery and daycare; a selection of the upcoming trade school classes; a schedule of visiting lecturers, musicians, poets, and actors; information about healthcare, which was free; exhibits at the art museum (abstract expressionism, what else); showtimes at the movie theater; a bus schedule. Most of these amenities seemed to be located around the plaza, in the center of which rose an impressive sixty-foot-tall wrought-iron statue of a shark. The style was abstract and deconstructed, the essential bits forming an outline, a skeletal framework. On closer inspection it seemed to have the body of a shark and the head of a satellite dish. Pigeons pecked at its feet.

I watched the Dumanians go about their lives on this slab of a settlement in the middle of a nowhere desert. I was struck by the uniform theme of the place: no matter in which direction I faced, my gaze was comforted by the expected, even when the buildings strayed from the characteristic cubist shapes. The library on one side of the plaza had a spectacular wall of reinforced glass through which I could see stacks and stacks of books, and people lost in the aisles, reading at tables, luxuriating in knowledge. I wanted to be placed there, among the history and art, the literature and philosophy. That's where I wanted to work on my buildings.

I noted the location of the bus stop, too, which I would be using in the morning to get to Factory 7A. It was made of glazed brick that curved into a half-shell, providing shade and a spine to rest against. Elsewhere there were signs pointing toward the theater, the playground, the agricultural center, and the museum. Nothing looked like an obvious place to ask about a city directory, and there were no mailboxes to speak of. I was dismayed. I was exhausted. I wanted to go home.

# FOUR

DUSK HAD SET IN by the time I returned to the Crescent. I passed a few people in the narrow hallway—we had to sidle past each other, our backs flat against the curving wall—who were off to begin night shifts doing who knows what. Two women and one man. The women wore those form-fitting utility jumpsuits. The man wore a herringbone suit; his hair was combed back against his scalp and wet. None of them smiled at me, though I smiled at them. They didn't seem happy, as Erich had described them. Erich, who had fully invaded my thoughts. I couldn't stop thinking about who he had been and who he had become. His transition from Eddy to Erich.

I let myself into my apartment. It was cool and dark. I hadn't closed the blinds in the living room when I left that morning, but it didn't seem to matter—this was a thoroughly insulated building. The window-wall looked out onto a hill patchy with yellowed grass and red dirt. The sun had sunk behind the hill many hours earlier. I ate a dinner of fruit and synthetic meat while sitting on an ottoman and staring at the clock above a sleek wooden credenza. It was only after I'd finished my meal that I remembered the gastrointestinal distress from earlier. It seemed to have gone and not come back. There was a speck of meat left on my plate. I held it between my thumb and pointer finger and examined it. It slithered in its grease.

After I ate and did the dishes, I decided to finally unpack the bag I'd been given. I suppose I felt that once I had unpacked, I was accepting that I was here for good, however long "for good" meant. I looked through the drawers and cabinets of the little apartment, searching for the best place for my clothes, and as I did so, I made a catalogue of the household supplies provided. The kitchen cabinetry held the usual accoutrement. Flatware and plates; cups made of rubbery, glasslike material, easily washed; pot and pan and hotplate; cooking utensils. The nightstand by my bed contained a pad of paper and a cheap, flimsy pen. The pad had Dumanian watermarks on each page. There was no bedroom closet—only a few racks of metal shelving that were attached to the wall. I would hit my head on one of them eventually. There was nothing in the bathroom. The mirror opened to a sepia-colored plastic cabinet for medicines and hygiene products. I'd have to get soap in town.

In the living area, the only piece of non-modular furniture was the credenza—synthetic wood, though whoever had put it together had stylized it: there was a pleasurable grain to the wood, interplay of light and dark where the boards connected in a jigsaw-like motif. Six drawers and squat, cylindrical legs at obtuse angles. I opened each of the drawers and the apartment filled with a realistic smell of pine. When I opened the bottom right drawer, something gave way in my hand. I pulled the drawer out, then palmed around the underbelly of the unit until I felt something papery. I detached a photograph that had been glued there.

The photo was black and white, on thick film stock, and showed what looked like a Bechstein grand in the corner of a divided room. The walls were fitted with two rows of equally sized, vertically standing columns of felt or carpet. The patterned hardwood floor had a crosshatching of wooden rectangles. The piano's lid was closed. Most of the light in the picture came from bulbs that weren't visible to the camera: inlaid, perhaps, in the beams that supported the ceiling. The light touched the tops of the felt rolls. In the back of the picture, the room split, but whatever lay beyond had been painstakingly removed from the photograph in the darkroom.

Nothing was written on the back of the photograph and it wasn't dated. I brought it into my bedroom and placed it in the nightstand drawer, alongside the pen and pad. Then I brushed my teeth and sat on the edge of the bed, crinkling something. I lifted my rear and found the map I had been using all day. It was in perfect shape, no longer blurred and stained by my sweat. Somehow even clearer than before.

I switched off the light. The sheets were soft, but the mattress, which had been feathery and accommodating before, was now thin and hard, as if it had degraded rapidly. I counted eight coils of springs digging into my back. I closed my eyes and thought about Professor Hallen. He was a tall man, with a blond down covering his arms. He kept his curly hair cropped above his ears. I could never get a read on his age; he could have been anywhere from forty-five to seventy. He had a high forehead and an unkempt, hircine beard that coated his throat and disappeared into his shirt collar. In one of his publications, which I remembered coming across by chance in the philosophy stacks one day, there was a photograph he'd taken of himself spread over two pages, with the camera visible on a tripod in the mirror. In the photograph, his shirt was off and his back to the camera. On his back there was a tattoo of a scroll with a curled top and bottom, and on that scroll, which extended from shoulder to shoulder and nape to buttock, neatly, was a representation of thirty-six religious icons in a grid. It took my breath away. Not only from the sheer feat of it, the pain and time and ink, but that a person I knew rather well could have markings like these buzzing just beneath the skin of his clothes.

The last time I saw him was the last day of the semester. Hallen surprised us with a bottle of quality Russian vodka. As he set twelve shot glasses on his desk and began to pour, he talked at length about the virtues of the course, of what we had accomplished by smashing headlong into the ugly vitriol and urbane cruelty of fascist texts. In that cramped and sweaty office of his—we met in his office and not in one of Barnova's collegiate redbricks or the English or History departments' carriage houses—we sat at a semicircle of smaller desks, watching the vodka rise quickly to the rims of the glasses, overflow. Though we were all of drinking age, there was still a thrill in this lapse of professorial, authoritative boundaries. I made eye contact with Hao, my closest friend in that class. He shot a glance past me at Sezim, sitting to my left—a Muslim from the Bloc who wore a hijab. All semester, Sezim had been the butt of Hallen's jokes. Playful barbs we took to be in good humor: knowing digs at Sezim's culture, the pointing out of equivalences between her religion—her *family's* religion, he liked to stress, as if her identities weren't her own—and the content of the texts before us. All done lightheartedly, with Hallen's smile hatching through the nest of his beard, as if to say: *naturally* fascism and Islam aren't the same, but this is the sort of thing *other people say*; I'm simply parroting the rhetoric, for this is a class on inciting language after all, isn't it? Sezim had smiled along with the rest of us as the temperature rose and our collars tightened.

Hallen's toast culminated with a reading of the poem that had been written on his chalkboard forty years earlier by one of the continent's greatest thinkers, a contentious figure in the sciences who at one time had worked out of this same office. Hallen often pointed to the poem, sometimes sang it in his startling, swampy bass—especially when waxing poetic about the state of the world. The poem meant nothing to any of us. It was the language of a theoretical physicist and fell on deaf ears among humanities majors who found our paths mostly through negation.

None of us could have cut it in the sciences. Our skills in math were mostly nonexistent, though I could get by well enough for architecture. The poem appeared to draw a comparison between the inevitable paths of electrons and the inevitable arcs of history and class struggle. But it only *appeared* to do that. There were nuances, jargon, subtleties I could never perceive. For me, this poem represented the limits of my intelligence. It haunted me.

The shots were poured. More than half of the bottle remained. Hallen began to pass them out, two at a time, walking to our desks and handing us our shots, then returning for the next two. When we all had our apportioned vodka, Hallen raised a shot of his own. *Prost*, he said. We raised our glasses and drank. A few students sputtered, vodka shooting out of their mouths. Sezim hadn't touched her glass. She had a broad face with sharp, dark eyebrows. Her cheeks were flushed. Hao leaned over my desk to get her attention. He offered his hand and smiled. He'd take the shot for her. Not exactly an act of selflessness, but a kindness nevertheless. Hallen materialized. He stood at my desk, his waist at eye level.

"You must toast with us, Sezim. On our last day. It's tradition."

"I'm sorry," she said. She was more than contrite, I remembered. She was apologetic, and she didn't have to be. "I can't."

"Of course you can," said Hallen. "It's a celebration." Hallen moved the shot, which had landed on my desk, back onto hers. "Go ahead, my love," he said. "Only one." He watched her expectantly.

Sezim looked up at Hallen. There was fear in her eyes, sure, but I thought I saw more than that. I saw hatred there, too. I looked up at Hallen, whose cheeks were red, and wondered if it hadn't been the day's first tipple.

One of the other students spoke up. "From the hand-book of Il Duce himself."

We all laughed and for a moment this seemed to break the tension. Hallen smirked at the student.

"How about this," said Hallen, turning back to Sezim, who sat straight-backed, her hands folded on her lap beneath the desk. "How about we all take the bloody shots so we all can pass the class?"

"Are you really going to fail me if I don't?" Sezim said. By now she was resolute.

He stared at her, letting several seconds elapse. No one spoke. The radiator popped and groaned. Then he laughed, an abrasive, braying laugh. His yellow teeth glowed under the fluorescent lighting. We all joined in, relieved. All of us but Sezim. I looked briefly at her hands on her lap, laced so tightly that the knuckles shone white.

The last thing that I remember of that day is an image of Erich.

It's there on the periphery of this memory, or more likely in the dead center of it, the black hole pulsing in the center of the galaxy, faint and faded, one of the chalk-board poem's electrons in an unstable state. I saw it and looked away as from an unforgivable sight, my mind in its grip, an icon of paroxysm. But I had seen it; I couldn't prevent it; it was right there. And now I was here, in bed, seeing it again, *willing* myself to see it:

Erich, hunched over his desk in the middle of the semicircle, when all other eyes were on Hallen and Sezim and the drama of the vodka. His back bowed and his eyes empty and sunken in the blue-black folds of his flesh, his long nose cleaving down his face, his mouth open, a spot of saliva breathing there. His hands beneath the desk like Sezim's—holding his erect penis, aroused by the violence, the surging power emerging through his pants, its head visible through the tunnel of his hands, right there, gazing out into the classroom from the shadows beneath the desk, palpitating,

its throbbing,

unblinking

eye.

I tried to sleep, trying both sides, back, stomach. I couldn't find comfort. The pillow felt like it was stuffed with tissue paper. Minutes passed. More minutes. At two in the morning, I heard a soft rapping. I got out of bed. My senses were heightened. I pulled on a robe and pressed my ear against the door, too afraid to open it. The sound came again, and I realized it was someone knocking on the door next to mine. Not for me. I felt such an acute sense of relief that I nearly collapsed. What was I so afraid of? I slouched back to the bedroom and got into bed, accusing myself of being a coward. Then, without totally realizing it, I was listening to an exchange taking place in my neighbor's apartment. There were two voices, one female, one male.

"Can I get you something to drink?" Her voice was quiet, timid. European. It was my neighbor.

"I'm fine, thanks."

Prolonged silence. Shuffling. Slight movement. Words muffled.

"I'm exhausted." My neighbor again. "I'm just tired."

"That's all right." His voice midrange, clear, British.

"Why don't you get into bed."

More silence.

"It's all right. If you don't like it, we won't. Easy. Very low stakes."

"Okay."

Shuffling. Footsteps. Coming toward me. Springs: a bed. I sat up gently, twisted my head, and placed my ear on the wall. I tried to form a map of the apartment from the sounds. It was identical to mine, I was sure, but maybe its inverse, which put our bedrooms on opposite sides of the same wall. Likely a design intended to reduce noise bleed between the main living spaces.

Shoes removed. More bedsprings.

"How do you want me?" More confident now.

"However you would naturally." He had the crystal cadence of the fancy English. For some this would be a turn-on. I wondered how the process worked here. An arrangement made ahead of time?

A bag unzipped. Shuffling. Zipping, unzipping.

"I like to be on my right side, with a pillow between my knees, curled up." Excited now. In control. "Like this.

## ZACHARY C. SOLOMON

I can't believe I'm saying this. You never talk about this sort of thing. It's so personal. Like a little baby, like this."

He got on the bed. Bedsprings wincing. These were twin mattresses. They were not accommodating for two. Creaking, bouncing.

She said, "Not like that. Put your arm here. Like this."

"Here?"

"Exactly. Now fold your knees deeper. Into mine. Imagine they are *glued* into the backs of my legs. They *cannot* be removed. Yes. Deeper than that."

"They don't go any deeper."

"Please," she said. "Yes. That's it."

"Do you want me to sing to you?"

*"Sing?"*

"I know many melodies and lullabies. I have a robust repertoire."

She laughed, disarmed. "That's sweet of you to offer. But I'd like to go to sleep now."

"Good night, little baby."

Laughing again, sleepy. That was a nice touch.
I fell asleep imagining the cushion of her comfort.

There was an Americanism I knew that went something like—*dress for the job you want, not the job you have.* A sad capitalist tautology we used to make fun of. If you don't already have the higher paying job, then you can't afford the nicer clothes. I needed to make a good impression if I was going to get out of manual labor and back into my original designation. I pulled my jacket on over a gray button-down shirt that I tucked into a pair of loose khaki trousers. I wanted to look like an architect, not a laborer. The jacket would strengthen the case I would make to the foreman and distract from the ill-fitting pants. The clothes that had been packed for me were a huckster's attire.

I ate quickly, left my apartment at seven, and walked with a few other commuters into Beau Gino Plaza. We congregated under the brick curve of the bus stop awaiting our transports. Some of those waiting with me were dressed in the gray utility jumpsuits I'd seen often. They were made of thick material, probably stifling in this heat, designed to prevent nicks and burns. If the people wearing them seemed undisturbed by the heat it was because they seemed undisturbed by anything, their faces drawn and inert in the morning fog. Others wore clothing more conventional for construction work and were chatting happily, holding thermoses of coffee.

The diversity of the group was astonishing to me. People speaking with accents I didn't recognize, from places I'd never been; peoples whose provenance I couldn't begin to guess. I wondered if this had to do with where Duma was situated geographically—whether it had been founded at the intersection of continents or along well-traveled roads. I thought back to my journey by train and bus, now a bit blurry, and how remote we truly were here. I didn't even know where *here* was. Nowhere at home—not even at Barnova, which attracted international scholarship—had I experienced such a Babel. Every single person looked like they belonged elsewhere.

Buses came every five minutes or so, old ones with faded red paint, dragging exhaust pipes through the dirt. Paper signs in the windows listed one of three destinations, but the codes were meaningless to me. I worked up the nerve to ask someone and was surprised to find that she didn't speak English despite the mandate. I wound up showing my assignment to a few people before I found one who could read. He was a short, hairy man with East Asian features. I wanted Route B, he told me. It arrived shortly after in a cloud of dust, like the buses before it. I piled on with six or seven others and sat in the next-to-last row on a bucket seat with frayed argyle fabric. We bounced off into the steppe. I felt every rock and divot in the road. The radio was turned up: some awesome Wagnerian movement.

Duma faded behind us, and beyond it lay a rocky expanse, hilly, the colors red clay and toasted yellow. Flowers blossomed from the cracks between the rocks—desert flora, spiny purple umbels motionless in the still air, stark white sand lilies, squat cacti. Particulates in the air. Sand. Gravel. At some point, far, far off in the distance, I saw a black house in the middle of the desert. I couldn't tell if it was painted black or had been charred by fire.

We crested a hill and a factory district appeared. Long, rectangular, industrial buildings arranged in rows, glass-fronted with concrete support beams and bifurcated windows. They all looked roughly the same, though some had domed roofs, others flat, and some were several stories tall. It was a desolate place, really. There was nothing except the factories, self-enclosed in a way that made them seem like they could be moved at any moment. Like they'd been plopped down from above.

The bus pulled over and we filed out into a small plaza. There were a few of the same concrete benches, along with some shops and a café. The plaza was lined with palm trees. Beneath one, a sharp-beaked bird tortured a scorpion. It was quite pleasant. A nice place to take a break, I thought. The buildings announced their numbers in massive block lettering above the entrances. I spotted 7A, walked over, stood in its shadow, and swelled with feeling, suddenly anxious about what the foreman would think of me—what the other workers would think of me. What if it didn't work out? What if they made me do...whatever it was they did in Factory 7A? What if I became ensnared in a bureaucracy that could take years to escape?

I would have to be strategic in my talk with the foreman, show him that my well-developed skill set was honed specifically for architecture, that it would be a shame to waste it on something menial. I inhaled sharply—the earthen smells, the dust, the warming air—and felt my stomach cramp. Nerves, I thought, or another bad reaction to the meat. Around me workers were entering their factories without hesitation. They knew exactly what they were doing. They seemed intent, motivated; their faces were sharp, almost beaked. I inhaled again, and then the glass doors parted and I entered. An atrium rose before me, topped by a skylight held in place with iron grillwork. I looked around in a daze. It was light and airy and modern, not at all the blue-collar workplace I was expecting.

"This way, sir."

A young man in a pressed suit stood by a door toward the back of the atrium. He gestured with a bow, a servant's posture. I followed him through the door and down a windowless hallway, a jarring transition from the air and light of the atrium. We arrived quickly at a green door marked *Site Manager*. He knocked twice and turned the knob, pushing it wide then holding it for me, his arm working hard against the weight. I thanked him and stepped inside. Another man stood from behind a desk and put out his hand.

"Matias Kamwendo," he said.

I approached the desk and we shook hands. He had long fingers with sharp nails that dug into my wrist. He was toweringly tall and quite thin, and he wore an olive green jumpsuit. His face was beautiful, with full, purple lips, an elegant nose, and blue-gray eyes that shone under arched eyebrows stuck in a peevish look. A desk fan with a metal cage blew dully across the room.

"Do you have a note for me?"

I fished the assignment out of my jacket pocket and handed it to him. He read it and nodded.

"The thing is, there seems to have been some kind of an error," I said.

"It says right here that you've been placed for manual labor." He pointed at the note with one of his long fingers, and I realized he had a British accent. "I don't see a mistake."

He sat, and I took that as my cue to sit, too. Other than the metal desk, the fan, and the two chairs, there was nothing else in the office. Only the door, four walls, and a horizontal sliver of a window cut into the concrete, through which beamed a bar of light.

"If there was a mistake—and I assure you there wasn't," said Kamwendo, "but if there was, then what is it exactly that you were expecting to do?" He folded his arms on the desk and leaned forward. His face was open, expressive—but those eyebrows.

"You see, the note says manual labor, but just because the note says it doesn't mean—you see, I am actually a trained—well, nearly—"

"Manual labor is satisfactory. There's an opening that would be perfect for a man of your figure." He assessed my body.

"I was supposed to serve as an architect. I was told—"

"Architecture? Here?" He chuckled. "You've seen the caliber of building here, haven't you? They don't bring in just anyone for a position like that. Between us, they tend to hire in-house."

"I could speak with the architecture board, if necessary," I offered. "I'm nearly finished with graduate studies—not quite, but..." I trailed off when his body language shifted. He seemed to have interpreted this as a threat. He took a pen out of his pocket and spun it on the desk. It settled between us, the nib pointing at me in accusation.

"We don't waste their time on trifles," he said. "You did do a vocational exam, didn't you?" Kamwendo leaned back and glanced at my assignment paper again.

"No," I said. I ran my hand across my forehead; it was slicked with sweat. I couldn't tell if I was losing my patience or losing my sense of equilibrium.

"We can do it however you want."

"The exam?"

"We should do it however you want to maximize your proficiency, efficiency, and output."

"I am here to be an architect!" I shot out of my seat, surprising myself. The blood rushed from my head. I leaned on the desk for support. Tears came to my eyes. He watched me calmly, let me sway. I sat down.

Kamwendo didn't bat an eye.

"This embarrasses both of us, Mr. Zelnik."

"I'm sorry," I said. The room spun. I felt ill—or worse.

I was losing track of the proceedings.

"Collect yourself, fellow."

I closed my eyes and took a deep breath, focused on the warm air that blew across my face as the fan oscillated.

Blood resumed its flow through my veins; the room settled; I became calm.

I was ready.

"There are areas that I'm more fluent in than others," I said. "Topics I'm more interested in."

"So, which is it?"

"Which is what?"

"Do you want to be assigned a placement or do you want to create one?"

"I am prepared to do—whichever is most helpful to the settlement?"

Kamwendo propped his feet up on the desk, crossing them at the ankle. His jumpsuit hadn't prepared me for the polished black loafers. I couldn't read his expression now. He seemed to have become frustrated with me, but the unreadable shape of his face, the arching eyebrows and wrinkled forehead, made him appear upset regardless of the proceedings. I didn't want to let him down, so I tried to explain myself again, but I was only talking in circles. He opened a desk drawer and rummaged through its contents, then closed it and looked at me. The conversation took on the feeling of an interrogation; his speech was interrogative; he was waiting for me to spill myself naturally. Give me enough room and I will falter. Give me enough space and I will flail through it to find its contours. I will smash into the contours of the space. I will break the space to find its shape.

At last, he interrupted my babbling.

"When we consider the widely-accepted limitations of the average worker and the material that she produces—a doctor, a farmer, a judge, for instance—and then when we consider the spectrum of their personage—their attitudes, their interests, their socioeconomic relations, for instance—we find that their work is a dire inadequacy, a failure on all fronts to address the full range of their creative faculty. Do you agree?"

"Of course. People shouldn't be limited—"

"Then how do you process the worker in a way that exercises all of her capabilities?"

"There are a few things that come to mind," I said. "You could ask her what she does for fun."

Kamwendo was quiet for a long time. I started to believe I had said something intelligent.

Eventually he said, "Like a date? You'd ask a question like that on a date."

"I suppose so, a bit like a date, yes."

"I see." He smiled wearily. "Here's what we're going to do," he said. "I'm going to send you down the hall to processing. They're going to fix you up with your placement, answer any more questions you might have, and show you to your workstation." Kamwendo stood, his chair wheeling backwards into the wall. "A pleasure."

"What if I'm not happy with my placement?"

He stuck his hand out and I quickly stood and accepted it.

"You'll do great," he said, as if productivity was happiness. He led me out by the elbow and pointed down the hall. The door closed before I could thank him.

I followed his directions and found the door to processing. I entered, was ushered into a concrete cubicle by a forceful woman in a white habit, and a moment later was face to face with Matias Kamwendo again. He shook my hand and bowed slightly, then took a seat behind the green desk, placing some files he had brought with him into a drawer.

"Hot in here, are you?" He reached below the desk and brought up a fan identical to the one from his other office, plugged it into a wall outlet, and switched it on. It began to whir in the same fashion.

"They have you doing double duty, huh?" I said jovially. I felt I could be casual with Kamwendo now that our relationship had traversed time and space. He was rooting around in the desk drawer, extracting file folders and papers, but he paused when I asked this and looked over at me.

"Pardon?"

"From before," I said. "Site managing *and* processing. That seems like a lot of moving parts."

"I'm not following you."

"You just sent me in here," I said. "I was with you in your office two minutes ago. Now you're meeting with me here in this room. It seems like a few too many repetitions in the bureaucracy."

"You weren't here two minutes ago," he said. He laughed a little, nervously, I thought, then put two fingers in his collar and tugged it away from his throat. I realized then that the jumpsuit he was wearing was a different color than the one he wore as Site Manager. That suit had been a dark, murky green; this one was a deep ocean blue.

"They make you change?" I said, louder than intended.

"I have to insist that we move on," he said. He gathered his files and folders into a pile, tapped them into order against the desk, and began to peruse them. I was certain now that I was being tested, which was fine with me. A test like this would prove my mettle; they would understand the real me, process me accordingly, and find my directive, which, naturally, would be architecture. I would become inessential. I would enter the paradigm.

"It looks here like there's an opening at Row F. You'll slot right in. How's that sound to you?" He placed the paper on the table and rotated it so I could see, placing one of his long nails on the exact spot. I knew I was supposed to look at the factory map, but I couldn't take my eyes off his face—the same blue-gray eyes under the same severe eyebrows.

"I want to be helpful," I said. "I was hoping to put my architecture degree to use."

Kamwendo sat back in his chair, his face drawn in consideration. "Row F is a bit like architecture," he said. "The parts look like little buildings. You fit them together—well, they fit much like a train on a track, the way the wheels sit in the grooves—no, I suppose it's a lot like architecture—do you know the Chinese Dougong? Yes, it's a little like architecture, interlocking parts and whatnot. You'll be very happy in Row F."

"Mr. Kamwendo," I said. "What's going on here? This isn't necessary, is it?" The calm I'd felt minutes earlier had evaporated, leaving only agitation—and dread.

Kamwendo pinched the bridge of his nose as if to make sure it didn't ooze across his face. "I'm having trouble."

"Is he your brother? Are you twins?" I didn't care if I was being nosy or unprofessional. If this was a test I would barrel straight through it, smashing its parameters, winning the evaluation through ambition and perseverance, my inability to be fooled, my brazen intuition. "If this is a mind game of some sort," I declared, "then I won't be taken."

Kamwendo met my gaze. "Can we sit here for a moment?" he asked.

I nodded. If he thought he could wait me out, could outlast my ambition, then he was in for a surprise. We both sat back in our chairs. I crossed my arms. He closed his eyes. I took the opportunity to further study his face. The more I examined, the less certain I became that he really was the same person as the foreman. My mental image of that prior person had already begun losing its definition. And when it occurred to me that I might have confused the two since they shared the same skin tone, that it was my own subconscious biases betraying me, I flushed, sweaty with humiliation. Suddenly it seemed possible that I had simply conflated two marginally similar looking individuals, negating both of their identities while masquerading as their ranked superior. I was mortified.

"Sir," I said. "I'm sorry if I offended you in any way."

Kamwendo—or whatever the processor's name was— looked at me, doubt in his eyes. "Offended?" He shook his head. "No offence taken here."

"That's good," I said. "Very good." My relief was massive. He was letting me off the hook. He was granting me a favor. Clearly, I now owed him one. Maybe a big one.

"Splendid," he said. He shook his head again, free of whatever had held him in place. "I'll show you to your workstation, then."

He rose, and I did, too, and together we walked out of his cubicle and back into the hallway. He walked quickly, his loafers clacking against the polished concrete floor, and I had to double my stride to keep up.

"Sir," I said. "Sir." He either couldn't—or wouldn't— hear me. "I'm not satisfied with the results of this conversation." He seemed to have mistaken my contribution for submission. But as we walked, I realized that this was to be how I would pay him back for forgiving me for mistaking him for someone else.

I vowed to myself then that whatever the job turned out to be, I'd put in tenfold the effort of my peers, prove to both the processor and Mr. Kamwendo that the assignment was all wrong, and in no time I'd be on the architecture board, doing good work. I was well on my way to a house of my own, a garden of my own. Well on my way to leaving my mark on Duma.

The processor made a turn, then abruptly pushed wide a door. It opened onto the factory floor, a long, bustling room with floor-to-ceiling glass windows that faced the main street. The room was divided into two columns of twenty or so rows of long, contiguous worktables, and men and women in gray jumpsuits stood or sat eight per table, four per side, working with parts and tools.

# FIVE

**N**O ONE LOOKED AT US when we entered. The dominant sound was metallic clanging. I lost track of the processor amid the stimuli for a moment, then caught his eye as he waited, arms crossed impatiently, at one of the worktables. I followed him to a worktable at the far side of the factory floor. He pointed down the row to an empty space at the table. It was window-adjacent; I would have a view of the main street, and access to sunshine and fresh air. My window seat clearly indicated that I had performed well enough.

"Here you are," not-Kamwendo said above the noise. "Best of luck." We shook hands. I held on a moment longer than was proper and looked at him intently, searching for a sign—of what? That he sympathized with me? That he understood my dilemma but, hey, there's nothing I can do? He seemed to get the point and winked at me before walking away.

I sat down on my stool and looked around the workstation. There were small parts arranged in tidy boxes along the metal table. The parts were pipes, or tubes—metal, or some other hard and shiny synthetic material—some colored hunter green, others plain silver. Some were bent into elbow curves, or L-shaped ones. Others were simple cylinders of various thicknesses. There were boxes of screws, bolts, washers. A brand-new toolset with screwdrivers, monkey and Allen wrenches, pliers. I looked across the table at the woman in front of me. She was tall and slender in her uniform, her dark hair tied up in a white bandana. She had the appearance of certain nomadic peoples who used to come through my former city seasonally. Her hands were smudged with black grease and her nose was concave. I tried to catch her attention, but she was too focused on her task, fitting smaller pipes into larger pipes, rotating them, peering through. When she was satisfied by the geometry of her part—some were complete at a full square, others finished the moment she extracted a part from a box—she threw it on top of a growing pile in a crate by her feet. I looked at my feet and found my crate. In the bottom was a printed list of parts I needed to assemble. It seemed simple enough; the list was long and itemized. There were 2,000 shapes to put together. I wasn't sure if that was the day's goal or the week's goal.

The worker to my right was engaged in the same activity. He was a much older man, in his seventies maybe, and after every third or fourth completed assembly he would take off his spectacles and clean them with an oily rag, which only made them oilier. He moved at a slower pace than the woman in front of me. Neither of them had acknowledged my presence when I sat down. I respected their concentration too much to interrupt their workflow for greetings.

Assembly was a cinch. After the first hour I could finish four assemblages in under a minute. The pipes had a coat of grease on them that easily transferred to my hands. By the time I realized it, there was already a grease spot on my slacks near the crotch. I paused for a moment, watching my coworkers. They were good at their jobs, efficient. The woman across from me was performing eight assemblies a minute. Twice as efficient as me. I wanted to beat her.

I worked harder and faster, feeling the sun on my face as it rose above the building across the road and arced onto the left side of my body. I didn't want to take my jacket off; I didn't want to be indecent. Sweat formed in my armpits and dripped down my torso. It ran into my eyes, but my hands were covered in grease, so I couldn't wipe my forehead. Instead, I used my cuffs, which was indecent. I was thirsty, but no one else appeared to be drinking water, so I didn't either. Occasionally, overhead vents pumped cool air into the factory, but I barely felt wisps of it. The coolness didn't make it down to us at Row F. It lingered in the rafters and dissipated.

I filled my first crate and then sat idly, watching the workers around me, waiting to see what they did with their completed assemblages. Finally, a worker at the end of my table picked up her full crate. I grabbed mine and followed behind her, walking down the aisle. I looked up at the factory ceiling, at the extraordinary lights that would eventually illuminate the room when the sun was gone. They were glass cubes attached to the ends of long and thin metal rods that hung from the ceiling every ten feet. They were beautiful to look at; a faintly bronze glaze coated their surfaces.

She led me to a conveyer belt where workers were carefully emptying their crates. I found a spot at the belt and did the same. It was even hotter here, deeper inside the factory, away from the windows that at least provided an intermittent breeze. Two of the workers near me were making small talk in thick Middle Eastern accents. I placed one assemblage after the next on the belt, watching them disappear into another room by way of a channel in the wall. When I had finished, I picked up my crate and turned, accidentally bumping into a worker with a full crate. He cursed at me, spilling his assemblages, and I ricocheted into the belt where the bottom of my jacket got caught in the gears. I shouted for help and a few workers came to my aid. They grabbed my arm as I tried to take off the coat—it was being ripped to tatters while pulling me toward a mechanism like a mouth sucking for the end of a noodle. They pulled hard enough that the coat split down the middle, leaving me on the floor of the factory wearing half a jacket, covered in sweat and grease, and bleeding from a cut on my hand, while the rest of my jacket disappeared into the jaws of the machine.

I was harshly reprimanded by one of the men who had come to my aid. "What do you think the uniform is for?"

"They didn't give me one," I said. I put my mouth to my hand and licked away the blood.

He laughed dismissively and went back to work. I returned to my table, took off the rest of the jacket, folded it neatly, and placed it beneath my stool. Then I buried my face in my hands and failed to suppress the grief surging through me. The exhaustion and fear I'd been trying to repress since arriving in Duma poured forth, brought about by the destruction of the one item I had with me that still tethered me to my home. I knew intellectually that Uncle wouldn't care—I doubted he would even remember giving the jacket to me—but still I felt a pyramid of guilt erupt from the land inside me. He would hate me now, just as he had all my adult life, yet even more so, even more powerfully, irrepressibly.

I lifted my face and looked around the worktable in Row F; no one paid me any heed. Had anyone even noticed my loss? Why were they so cruel?

My motivation to outwork the woman across from me was gone. All I felt was dried up and faint. Sweat stains had blossomed all over my shirt—in sagging pools beneath my armpits, in a dark face across my stomach. I was dehydrated. But I didn't want to get up again or waste any more time on myself and my self-pity. So I resumed working, more slowly, making my assemblages and filling up my crate. The light cascading through the windows started to darken, and this was a relief, as it meant the day was nearly over—but when I looked at the clock on the far wall, I realized that it was my vision darkening, not the daylight. I concentrated harder on assembly, finally refilling my crate. I thought about the destroyed jacket beneath my stool. How long it had taken to grow into it.

When I stood to deliver my crate to the conveyer, my knees gave way and I collapsed onto the factory floor.

I woke up in a cool, quiet room on a medical examination recliner. The wallpaper was off-white with a repeating floral pattern—daisies wrapped in red bandages. It was a pleasant image, and more color than I'd seen anywhere else so far. My arm was hooked to an IV drip. I watched the translucent liquid quivering in its tube and felt relaxed. There was no attendant nurse. Just me in the chair, a glass cabinet full of medical supplies, and the blissful air droning through a ceiling vent. I was still lightheaded but experienced it now as a sublime passivity: I turned my head to watch the hairs on my wrist flutter gently, almost imperceptibly, in the softly blowing air. The air came in waves, ebbing and flowing across my face, and each time it flowed my skin goose-pimpled. I couldn't imagine ever leaving this room, or shifting my body, ever again. My eyes closed and I had a sensation of remembering this exact moment in the concurrent timeline of another universe. I shivered all over, full of happiness.

I must have dozed off. After a time, I realized that my eyes were open again. I also realized that I was hearing a strange noise. A buzzing, a cable of electricity—loud like a zapper, but persistent, a seamless wire of sound with the nettling quality of fluorescent lighting. It was everywhere, but specifically the everywhere outside of the examination room. I slipped the IV needle from my arm and lowered my feet to the floor. Then I put my ear to the door and listened. All I could hear was that sound. I opened the door a crack, then a bit more—I was somewhere in the factory still. I could hear through the buzzing the clanging sounds of conveyance and assembly. Down the hall I went, following the buzzing until it became concentrated outside of a door marked *Basement C*. I pushed through the door and went down the stairs, descending into darkness. Four flights cut by cones of yellow light. And then another door—*Basement C*. I lingered for a moment and experienced a shudder of clarity—why was I following this sound? What was I doing? I was aware of a lack of awareness on my part, aware that I was powerless against it. I thought it was a strange experience, having a mind; I thought it was a strange experience that it's the mind who has a mind, not me. My mind wanted to follow the buzzing; who was I to say no?

When I entered, the buzzing became so loud that I had to cover my ears, like a boy blocking out the sounds of his arguing parents. The room was full of brown cardboard boxes, strewn at random, piled five or six high, unmarked and heavy. A single yellow ceiling light gently swayed in air currents from a nearby vent. I heard the indistinct murmur of a radio playing static. The boxes formed something like a labyrinth, which I began to navigate. It occurred to me that there was no way I could have heard a radio—the buzzing was an overwhelming, sense-devouring wall of sound. And yet I heard it: static. I kept wading through the boxes, following my ears and the alien sensations in my body. A box I didn't see tripped me, and I fell into one of the towers, sending boxes toppling to the floor.

Something metal in them made an awful, resounding crash. But I was getting closer to the source of the buzzing sound. I pulled myself back to my feet and pressed on.

Finally, I came to a clearing in the boxes and saw something extraordinary. Clustered around a metal trapdoor on the ground, there were a dozen or so cylindrical, translucent lamps, each with a bulb suspended in its center. The skin of the bucket-like lamps glowed drearily, illuminating strange vascular maps. Each one was sui generis, lopsided in its own particular, organic way as if slouching, and fifteen to twenty inches tall. They were organized haphazardly around the trapdoor, a four-by-four-foot metal hatch with hinges along one side. An aura of light, radiating.

I walked gingerly between the lamp-like forms, walking through, it became clear, a field of art. Either a single holistic piece, or thirteen or fourteen individual ones. The other lighting in the room, I realized, was museum lighting—the ceiling fixtures were trained at off angles to avoid direct exposure and to curtail glare.

I was very moved by the work. The organic materiality of the forms touched me on a human level; I felt that I was among friends, or even family. My own flesh and blood. The more closely I looked at the forms, the more the lamps' "shades" resembled human skin: a bacterial tapestry of blemishes, birthmarks, pimples, and moles. I got on my hands and knees so I could look more closely at the forms, which were now vibrating at an almost imperceptible frequency—yet I saw it, I saw the vibrations. I drew the back of my hand down the body of a form, felt the imperfections in its skin, the bumps and cuts, the sorrow and lassitude. I put my nose to the skin and inhaled: the scent of hair, unwashed. The odor made me dizzy, and I lost my balance, crashing into one of the forms. I quickly righted it, grateful that the sturdy construction was unharmed. Fixing it back into place, I noticed words stenciled onto the concrete.

### Are You Good Enough

Miriana Grannoff

Fiberglass, halogen bulbs, resin, miscellaneous material

Of course! A Grannoff original right here in the basement of Factory 7A! An astonishing development: I pictured her striving to place art in each factory, to show that art was not to be commodified but shared freely, disseminated to inspire the workers and to beautify the workplace.

It seemed that after all these years Grannoff was still experimenting with daring forms. The lampshades, by resembling human skin, appeared to manifest an ethical exigency. The work argued that one couldn't make progress without sacrifice—by creating an epidermal fabrication we see how the work demands the sacrifice of the body for the creation of light and shadow. The question is uncomfortable: Would we each be willing to give up some of our sacred corporeality to produce a thing we require to live—light? To sacrifice a degree of bodily integrity for the advancement and comfort of humankind? I felt accused: If called upon, I was not sure I could be decent or principled enough to make such a sacrifice from my own substance. Yet did I expect it from others? Was I willing to admit that either all bodies were equally valuable—or that all bodies were equally worthless?

I wasn't surprised to see this interrogative side of Grannoff's work. In our Barnova days, Grannoff had been consumed by questions of moral certitude and obligation, assigning us artist manifestos to pour over, championing texts from opposing viewpoints. To her, life was only worthwhile if it was leashed by a kind of rageful, intractable dogma. Although she was a leftist, she had a great deal of respect for the other side when it showed enough conviction, and subsequently was loathed by her comrades and adored by her rivals. She worshipped righteous rage above all else. The timbre of the message overshadowed the message itself. Her most common critique of her students' work was that they weren't passionate enough, that the artist came across as complacent and spineless. She had no problem humiliating students in front of the class, attacking their canvases with visceral critiques of workmanship and message, sometimes becoming so heated that she might destroy the work herself in a fit of violence. She was never without her black mohair beret, from which untamable gray hairs emerged like yearning vines. In the winter, she wore a self-designed parka made of thick, dreadlocked ostrich hairs that sprouted like limbs. It was stained all over in paint. We admired her despite her abuse; her praise compensated for her criticism; we lapped it up like warm, fresh milk.

## A BRUTAL DESIGN

When the academic purge began, she became more vocal than ever, protesting in front of the president's office with art professors and her coterie of devoted students, staging actions that doubled as protest art pieces that she made sure were recorded and catalogued. One day her protestors arrived wearing masks of burlap, with X's painted in bloody red across the fabric. Grannoff wasn't in a mask—I suppose she wanted to be seen. I watched through the windows of a public study room that overlooked the quad, safe behind the clouded window glass, absently feeling the vulgarities hollowed into the composite wood desk. I would have been out there with them if I hadn't been so afraid.

She was fired in the end. Off to South America.

I sat among the forms, contemplating her work—wondering how word of Duma had reached her, how she had reached Duma—when I realized the buzzing sound had returned, or rather, it had always been there, but now I noticed it again. It was terrifically loud, emanating from the hatch in the midst of the forms. I crawled over. The buzzing ceased when I touched the handle, as if the electrical current from my hand cancelled out the current of noise. I lifted open the hatch, which took all my strength, and let it fall to the cold cement floor with a tremendous crash.

I peered over the edge. I was looking down at a sea of carpet—faded, pastel-yellow carpet. A stench of mildew wafted up and jarred me; I pulled my head away and coughed, then looked again. I couldn't see as well as I wanted, so I got on my hands and knees and started to lower my head into the hatch. If I could just see beyond the shaft, if I could see just a bit more of the distance...I lowered my body further, extending like an eel through a tube, until my legs were lifted off the ground and I was angled downwards. More yellow carpeting came into view, more mildew spores into my nose. Beyond, I could see a darkened doorway and nothing more.

I could have let go. I could have dropped down, gone further. But something stopped me. I was vaguely aware of activity in my subconscious, an alert, warning me against falling. A recessed voice said that Uncle wasn't down there. That I wasn't allowed to be free until I found him.

I extracted myself but hit my head hard on the edge of the shaft. I fell back, clutching my skull, and the buzzing came roaring back, louder than ever. I covered my ears and squeezed my eyes shut, curling into a ball. My head felt like it might collapse in on itself. I pictured the indentions at my temple being sucked further inside, oblong, hourglass, further inside, oblong, hourglass, oblong, hourglass.

I was grabbed and pulled backwards and upwards, onto my feet, away from the hatch door and the smell of mildew. A pair of men in jumpsuits like Kamwendo's took me by the elbows and forced me up the stairs. I was lightheaded, close to losing consciousness, filled with regret—why hadn't I gone down into the shaft? It was fading behind me and I tried to resist, to go back and fling myself onto the carpeting below, run past the darkened threshold into the unknown. Instead I was prodded back through the hallways of the factory, past the med room, through the lobby, and out into the evening of the factory settlement.

I emerged. Took a deep breath. Looked at the stars. A surge of serenity coursed violently through me. And then I felt fine. Mollified. Home. The moon was a butter-yellow crescent split by a serpentine wisp of cloud. A few stars blinked in the purple sky. I sat by myself in the brick enclosure of the bus stop. A sundial stood uselessly in the center of the plaza. I wondered how long it had been since the last bus. No one was around, though I could see a few people blowing off steam in the café. Eventually a bus rumbled to a stop and I got on, its lone passenger. I was too tired to make small talk with the driver. He didn't seem to mind. He had the radio set to a talk station, but it was in a language I couldn't understand—against the rules, I thought. Bouncing over the rocky terrain reminded me that I hadn't eaten since breakfast. I decided I'd wander around Beau Gino Plaza and find something to eat. I spotted a cafeteria when we pulled in and made a beeline for it, glad to not have to search.

It was crowded inside—a brightly lit bunker of a building, with a long line of people in their work clothes holding trays and shuffling through a buffet. I grabbed a tray and joined the queue, accepting servings of fruit and meatloaf and a steaming bowl of fish stew. Long tables with low benches were arranged in the dining space. I sat at the end of a table of quiet loners and quickly dipped a crust of bread into the fish stew, then sucked the juice out of the dough. With my other hand, I cut into the meatloaf and shoveled a portion into my mouth. It was hot and wet with small crunchy bits that cracked like peppercorns. The fruit was mango and orange slices floating in a dish of their own liquid. Eating with my head down, nose inches from the tray, I had to remind myself to breathe between bites. I felt like an unsociable animal on its way to satiation.

Finally, I paused to savor the last bite of fish—a rich, silvery-gray morsel of flesh—and looked up. The others at my table were chowing down zealously. I scanned them, and then the other diners in the room. Most people were eating in groups of three or four, conversing gaily, being friends. Over by the window, I watched a group engaged in a three-way game of Alonzo Alonzo, linking their arms, wrapping their hands around the others' biceps, and squeezing at random to create a chain-reaction of muscle spasms. For the reaction to work, you have to time the squeezes one right after another, and you only have a window of a millisecond to get it right. If you nail it, your biceps begin to twitch in rhythm and don't stop until you release from the game. We used to play it at Sizenko Gymnasium.

One of the three players was much taller than his friends. His long neck shot out of his suit collar like an oak among reeds. It was Matias Kamwendo. I was impressed to see a Site Manager eating at a cafeteria like this. Or was he a Processor? Or were they in fact two different people? I still couldn't say. I definitely would have pegged Site Manager Kamwendo for a more elite dining situation. I supposed it could be that Duma didn't believe in class separation, like Erich had intimated when he said they'd moved away from private dwellings. I looked around at the building, thinking I'd see vestiges of a fancier eatery, but nothing. No crown molding, no embellishments. Evidently, eating was not recognized as a fine art. Well, be it Site Manager or Processor, I didn't want to miss my chance to do a bit of toadying. I placed my tray in the chute and strolled confidently over to Kamwendo's table.

"Excuse me," I said. "I'm sorry to interrupt your spirited game, but I wanted to thank my friend here for his help today." They looked up at me, their arms interlinked in a triangle of friendship. Eventually, Kamwendo realized I was speaking to him. He broke free of the game and stood, looking around. In the clear cafeteria light, I could see the ridges of his cheekbones and the oily plate of his forehead. I had forgotten how striking he was.

"What's that, friend?"

"I just wanted to express my gratitude for what you did for me today." I tapped my temple. "I'm a fast learner. The proof is in the parts. I nearly matched my neighbors, and it was my first day. I just thought you'd like to know, in case there are other opportunities. I've figured out the system already! You'll notice. I'll work my way up. Watch out," I joked. "You saw the right opportunity for me."

Kamwendo's friends giggled. I ignored them. Brown-nosing probably wasn't seen that often in Duma, but I didn't want to work in assembly for another week, let alone forever. Kamwendo looked down at his friends, rubbing the back of his neck with his massive hand.

"You're having me on," he said. A smile stretched across his face. "That's a good one. You got me. I've learned my lesson." He put one hand out palm down, then slapped it playfully with the other. His tone changed then, and he grew timorous. "I suppose, though, that I ought to be the one thanking you."

"Me?"

"I get it," he said. "You're being the bigger man. I'll be a big man too, then. I can say it: Thanks for taking the hit for me. Rahul was on my back about the mix-up with the ribbon and cartridge shipments. If you hadn't claimed responsibility for it, he would've found the delivery reports sooner or later and seen that I'd signed for them. He would've come after my head. You know how he is. If it weren't for you, I'd be in the desert in one of those bloody factories, my fingers bloody little stumps. You saved my ass. I'll be honest," he said. "I thought you were going to save this one for a rainy day when you could use it against me. The fellows here thought I needed to send you a fruit-cake to keep you quiet. I was sure it'd take more than a lousy fruitcake. But I'm grateful we could settle it here. I congratulate you on being the bigger man."

He put out his hand for a shake, but I didn't touch it. Was it too much to ask to have a simple exchange with this man? Why had I even bothered if he was just going to fuck with me again? I threw up my hands in defeat and walked away. Kamwendo's friends broke out in hysterics behind me. I pushed through the cafeteria doors and into the plaza. I was exhausted. A shiver ran through me, and I remembered that my jacket was gone. Both halves of it now. I had left its remains in the factory. I crossed my arms and walked briskly across the plaza and onto the street that led back to the Crescent. I pictured Kamwendo and his friends doubled over in their friendship triangle, wheezing at my naivete, ribbing each other. I was halfway home when I heard footsteps. Kamwendo was sprinting after me. He came to a stop, hands on his knees and panting.

"Look," he said, out of breath. "I really wasn't having you on back there. I'm grateful for what you did, Resnick. That's all. I don't want any bad blood between us, do you understand? And don't lord it over me, all right? I'm doing the right thing. Meet me halfway."

"You could at least have the decency to remember my name."

"Stop it. I'm trying to be serious with you. I don't want any funny business between the two of us. No more 'friendly rivalry' or any of that nonsense. Pals. What do you say? I'm tired of the fight. I'm hanging up my gloves. Okay, Resnick? Okay?"

"No," I said. "It isn't funny anymore." I was ashamed to find myself close to tears. I wanted to be home. I could see home curving into view at the end of the path. Soon I would be nestled inside among the modular furniture. I tried to take a deep breath, but it came up shallow. "Mr. Kamwendo," I mustered. "I do hope you consider my plan to approach the board of architecture seriously. I have every intention of seeing through the reason for my presence here in the first place." I was astonished by the words coming out of my mouth, felt that I was witnessing a schism of some kind, a departure of the frightened part of me from the mothership. I wanted to wrap my jacket tightly around myself, but the jacket was gone. "Goodbye, Mr. Kamwendo," I said. "I will see you tomorrow at the factory." I turned to leave but he caught my arm.

"Wait—what did you say?"

"Good night."

"Who is Kamwendo?"

"Matias Kamwendo," I sighed. "That's you. I'm Zelnik. We met today for the first time. When I reported for my first day of work this morning. We met twice, actually. The second time we met, you pretended we hadn't met before. But you don't remember, do you? Your policy is that you never remember. You keep on with the illusion. Completely ridiculous, this juvenile gestapo crap. I am very tired. I get what you're doing. I won't stand for it. Good night. I will see you tomorrow—unless you pretend not to remember then, too."

I began to walk again, but he caught up next to me and matched my pace, grabbing my elbow and tugging me to a stop.

"You're saying you came over to my table to thank me for something other than what happened with the shipments?"

"I came over to thank you for my placement at the factory. To show you that I take my work seriously. But if you really want to know the truth, the work is beneath me."

"I don't work in a factory," he said. "I'm at the pier. My name isn't Kallendo or whatever. My name is Richard

# A BRUTAL DESIGN

Winger. I work at the bloody pier. And you look exactly like my coworker Resnick."

I stopped and looked at him. Really looked at him. He really was Matias Kamwendo. He had to be. The same pronounced, regal nose. The full lips, the eyebrows set in irritation. I looked carefully into his eyes. They were round with hazel irises and inflamed, forking blood vessels. Exhausted eyes. We stood on the path just the two of us, meekly lit by a yellow streetlamp. In the yellow, his skin was a kind of jaundiced brown. He was beautiful. But after ten seconds or so it occurred to me that he was studying me, too. I became aware of the pressure of his gaze—his eyes, it turned out, were looking at my eyes. His pupils jerked back and forth like he was dreaming. He was looking at my eyes, my temples, my forehead, the bridge of my nose, maybe the nose itself, the long vale that lightly bifurcated it, the elevation in the center from a childhood accident; my reddened cheeks that always flushed from the weather, from embarrassments; the dip beneath my nose; my own pair of full lips and the prickly brownish-red hairs that grew all around them. I wanted to go back to staring at Kamwendo from my position of innocence, before I knew he was staring at me. Watch him without awareness that he was watching me. A sublime liberation of the self. But then to notice him watching me, objectifying me, comparing me to his Resnick, *negating me*. I was no longer myself; I became what Kamwendo saw as me. I felt myself shrinking into my face. I lost track of my body and melted into his eyes. I would say that it was a kind of falling in love, a total abandonment of the self in the gaze of another. But it was also displacement, a radicalized reformation of the self, predicated wholly on his subjective projection. I was no longer myself: I was only the seen and the not seen. And then I felt that he was seeing too much, like a mentalist who unearths your most private secrets by observing a twitch of your nose or the set of your mouth. How could I know whether Kamwendo possessed this gift, whether he could see through me to my fantasies, know me to my bones, go straight through to the unreachable kernel of Me?

How dare he.

I averted my eyes. We stood in silence, avoiding each other.

"There's a pier?" I asked.

Wind in the trees.

Winger exhaled, his posture slackening. "Yeah. West of here. About forty minutes on the bus."

"I didn't know we were that close to the ocean."

He mumbled something about catching the odor of it on windy days. And that was that. We shook hands and said goodnight. Winger said he'd see me around, and I guessed he would, in one way or another.

# SIX

HOME AT LAST. I crawled into bed without my usual pre-sleep routine, not even bothering to remove my clothes. I shut my eyes and waited for sleep, thinking it would come swiftly. Instead, my waiting generated a noise. A waiting noise. A buzzing anticipation of sleep. I listened to the tinnitus and tried to remember what had interested me in architecture in the first place. My old school, Sizenko Gymnasium, brand new when I entered as a fourteen-year-old. They'd built it from an old blast-furnace equipment factory. A block of steel and metal and concrete. The classrooms were boxes arranged in a circle around a common area and had glass walls so I could see other students in other boxes, doing workshops or learning music or calculus; or I could look outside, at the so-called moat and one of its wooden bridges and the forest beyond. The glass had transparent maps and tables and inspirational quotes etched onto it to prevent your mind from wandering or from watching the other students too much. But you could still see. That was the point. There was no way to approach the building without being seen by guards and teachers and administrators and students. It was a gorgeous school. Completely modern. A scholastic panopticon. The moat had two bridges, one on each side of the building. The water was deep and breathing, full of algae, Japanese koi, the gentle drifting of green lake life. This was the building that had made me fall in love with architecture. It was the first time I'd seen what a building could do for people, how form followed function, putting organizing principles to work—not in the name of money, but in service to humanity.

I wished I could remember the unit we were studying at Sizenko on the day of the guns. It was Mr. Radzinski's class, that I knew, which was biology. Dear Uncle, you would have remembered the shirt I wore that day. It was one of Dad's. You hated when I wore it, the purple tailormade shirt with flared cuffs. You told me it made a fool of me to wear it, which only made me want to wear it more.

It was early in the day. Eight in the morning, ten minutes into first period.

Were we studying molecules? I could make out symbols on the blackboard. But I could also picture the ligature *Æ.*

They came out of the forest. In my mind there were twelve of them, but who knows how many there really were. Bandanas tied around their heads—I could see them from my desk. Red and black bandanas that covered their mouths and noses. Camouflage, flak jackets, fatigues, army-issue boots, and rifles slung over their shoulders.

The principal's panicked voice through the PA. I can't remember his name. Isn't that funny? It wasn't even that big of a school. Maybe three hundred of us. We had done drills, countless drills. He cut the lights to the building and we hid under our desks as instructed. The locks engaged in the doors, a thick metal thunk. They couldn't get in.

Why don't I remember how it felt?

The principal's voice was a running chatter in the background. He had called the police. He reassured us. They couldn't get in. Remember your training. Nobody move. Nobody do anything provocative.

They came down the hill and stopped at the moat. The bridges had already been pulled. There was no way across the moat without swimming and it was a considerable span. They stopped at the edge of the water in formation. In unison they took the rifles from their shoulders and pointed them at our window. It was our window in particular. We were unlucky in that way, to be in the classroom facing the forest.

Then they just stood there, rifles trained at us. They didn't shoot. The glass was bulletproof, of course. Our school was built with exactly this in mind. All the money, the architectural and environmental principles that formed the basis of its design. Did it matter?

They stood there for a few minutes. I don't know how I could see them while I was under the desk. I must not have been hiding under it. I must have been watching. Through the glass, through the etching of the map of the world: the brown and black of the rifles, the barrels of their guns little black holes in the cloudy contours of the map. Why didn't they shoot? Was it only a demonstration? A reminder that they could kill us all, *if they really wanted to?*

They scattered, running back into the forest and disappearing. The police arrived shortly afterwards.

Do you remember what happened next, Uncle? We got the rest of the day off. They released us into the city. I was terrified to leave the school. Why would we leave? The school was the safest place for us. But they made us. They spent all that money and used all those minds to build a safe school and then they didn't let us stay in it. They sent us into the wild. I took the bus home. I didn't know where you were. Home by myself for hours, I got into bed and cried. When you came home and I told you what happened, you said it was a healthy experience. That's how you described it: healthy. Later, you let slip that you had heard about it from the news shortly after it happened. You knew I would have come straight home. You knew I was there by myself.

I wish I had said these things to you years ago instead of now saying them—practicing saying them—in my head. Maybe when we find each other in Duma I will tell you the rest.

I felt myself falling into sleep, but again something shook me. I had a sudden urge to see about something. I switched on my lamp, reached into my nightstand, and took out the photograph I had found in the credenza of the room with the piano and the rolls of carpet along the walls. This time I looked at the carpet in the photograph.

It was a black and white photograph, but I had a terrible, uncanny sensation: I knew, without proof, that the carpet was yellow. The same carpet I'd seen through the shaft. In the room beneath the ground. I don't know how I knew it, but I was sure of it. It was a fact that stood. A fact that mattered.

The next morning, I got to 7A early and made sure to stop by the front desk in the factory atrium to get a uniform. I was pointed in the direction of the inventory hallway and found the room for apparel. It wasn't difficult to find a jumpsuit my size, and in fact I felt that it rather flattered me, flattening my belly while emphasizing whatever muscular terrain I had left over from my Barnova sporting days, before my participation was disallowed. It was a khaki-green polyester suit with a zipper that ran from neckline to waist. The color brought out the brown in my hair. I ran my hands over my abdomen and felt attractive. It itched terribly.

It took a few wrong turns to find my way back to the factory floor, but when I did, I was among the first to arrive. I took some pleasure in this. The conveyor belt wasn't running yet; the overhead lights were still warming up. I found my stool and looked around to see if the ripped half of my uncle's jacket was still there. It wasn't. This saddened me, but I had work to do, so I started on the day's list of assemblages. I made it through a dozen or so before the wind left my sails. What was the point of this? What were these configurations *for?* By then my row had filled up with the same workers from yesterday. The older man was clearly senile. I didn't want to think about how long he had been sitting at this particular stool doing this particular work. A machine himself, he had been compiling assemblages for years and years, knuckles engorging, bones eroding. I pictured popping his knuckles with a sewing needle. I leaned over toward the woman in front of me with the white bandana. She was working intently, and at first I thought better of breaking her concentration. But what difference would it make? This was work that required no concentration, only stamina.

"Excuse me," I whispered. I said it a few times before she looked up. When our eyes met, she jumped.

"Hi?"

"Do you know what these are for?" I glanced down the table to make sure no one was listening, but it occurred to me that I had no good reason to be paranoid. Just because people didn't make conversation while they worked didn't mean that I couldn't. I hadn't been given any rulebook.

"Not a clue," she said. Her hands were working, compiling, locking. Still, she was looking at me.

"How long have you been here for?"

"The factory? Two or three years, I would think. It's pointless to keep track of it, so I don't."

"Why is it pointless?"

"It's not about time." She smiled, and her lips rose like a curtain to reveal small and crooked denticulation. "At least, I don't think it is."

"You've been assembling these parts for two years and you don't know what they're for?"

"We've got our theories," she said. "Jan thinks the work is the product and the product is the byproduct." She looked pointedly over at the old man, who was oblivious to our conversation. "Personally, I think they're all plumbing bits. For sinks and showers." I picked up a couple of parts—an elbow piece and a bracket—and idly played with them while she spoke. Water could travel through these parts. It seemed plausible. "Really, though," she said, "nobody knows for certain." She smiled like she was in on a secret. "Jan says it's all part of an elaborate piece of art. I think he's off his rocker."

I looked at Jan, who was already falling asleep on his assemblage.

"Thanks for the information," I said. I felt old-fashioned. The work was the product and the product was the byproduct? Was it too much to expect to understand the purpose behind their work? I looked around the factory and saw all the workers hunched over their tables, diligently assembling. There were worse ways to spend your time, I guessed. I couldn't pretend to know what compelled these people to care about their jobs.

While I knew it would be fruitless, I couldn't help but ask her if she had seen my uncle. I described him to her, and she made a show, maybe for my benefit, of racking her brain. She seemed to drift off into her mind. I was about to return to my own assembling when she spoke up.

"I'm sure I know him." Her expression took on a mystical configuration. A seer's face. "I'm sure I've seen him at the café."

"The café? Where is the café?"

"There's one in every plaza."

"Which one did you see him in?"

"This one, perhaps." She pointed to the window. I followed her finger to the plaza where the bus stop was located. "Sometimes I wander, though. When I'm on my break."

I didn't remember seeing anyone take a break yesterday.

I worked for a while longer, making slow progress down my daily assembly list. Mostly, I watched the other workers in the room with me, hunched at their tables, hands moving automatically, chasing salvation. The clangs of metal echoed off the concrete factory ceiling, making a kind of pleasant cacophony. I liked the music of the pipes. But the more I worked, the less I cared. I thought back to the indoctrination I'd been given on my first morning in Duma, that woman's passionate manifesto of Dumanian ideology. What ideology? The word belied the dead faces I saw surrounding me.

The sun had crested the factory across the street, and the room was now sweltering. I still hadn't seen anyone break for lunch, but I decided to brave it. What would be more humiliating? Being the first to leave for lunch—or losing consciousness again?

I rose timidly from my stool and wandered back through the factory and into the main atrium, looking around for a drink. There were no water fountains in sight, so I left the factory and walked into the central plaza, which was empty except for a few workers sitting on the concrete slabs in the shade of palm trees, tossing rocks at the scorpions in the courtyard. I walked along the perimeter, gazing into the shop windows: factory-appropriate apparel; tailor and seamstress; stool cushions; first aid; hanging crescents of cured sausages. Meat—that's what I wanted. I opened the shop window and a little bell chimed pleasantly. There were a few people enjoying sausages with mustard and sauerkraut, but they were eating alone at their own tables and I didn't feel like disturbing them for lunchtime small talk. My uncle was not there. I ordered a sausage, then took my platter to the window counter and ate greedily while I watched the sun bake the plaza. I cleaned my plate, sopping up the remains of the sauerkraut and mustard with my heel of black bread and savoring the juices from the wet and pillowy insides before washing the bread down with several cups of water. When I finished, I went to pay the young clerk behind the counter, a woman in a butcher's apron smeared with blood, but when I got there, I realized I didn't have any money. Henry had taken my wallet.

"How do I pay?" I asked.

"Sooner or later," said the clerk.

"I mean, I'd like to settle up."

"I thought you wanted a joke," she said. She looked up from her notepad and we locked eyes; her expression changed. "Have you been here long?"

"It's my second day at work."

"Lunch is free to the workers." She scribbled something down, ripped the sheet from the pad, and handed it to me. The little paper simply said *sausage*.

"What do I do with this?"

"Whatever you want," said the clerk. "Eat it for all I care." She turned to the counter behind her where loose meat needed casing. It looked more like the synthetic meat in my fridge than I'd realized. I glanced over my shoulder; the other diners were staring at me.

I asked her if she knew my uncle. I described him for her. She didn't have any tips on how I could find him.

"It's possible he comes here to eat," I said.

"A man eats in a restaurant. Congratulations."

The bell rang at my exit.

I stood in the sunshine and took a deep breath, thinking about the protein flowing through my blood. The sun bore down on me from overhead, but a bank of clouds was sailing along the plain. Soon it would blot out the sun, bring a breeze through the factory windows, maybe even rain.

I wasn't ready to go back inside. I wanted to look around a bit more and see if I could get lucky running into Uncle. At the very least, I felt the need to stretch my legs, get a bit of exercise. If this was going to be my routine from now on—sleep, eat, bus, factory, bus, eat, sleep—then I would need to be conscious of my health. I didn't want to become misshapen. A lap or two would do me good—raise my heart rate, bring a prickle of healthy sweat to my brow. I could explore one of the other plazas, maybe peek into the other cafes. I looked both ways down the avenue. The factories were like massive steel anvils. I walked east.

At the next avenue there was only more of the same: another broad and dusty street lined with factories, another plaza. Same shops, too. Same tailor and seamstress, same sausages hanging in the window. I cupped my hands against the glass and looked in; similar haggard workers looked out. None of them was my uncle. I walked into the center of the plaza and pictured myself from above: a black speck plotted in the grid of industry. I was reminded of an old memorial I once saw in my city, a gridded arrangement of marble rectangles of varying heights and elevations. But it wasn't a memorial when I saw it—it had been de-memorialized. The group for whom it had been built objected to their representation, to the vagueness, and commissioned the city to open the intention of the memorial up to the Universal Tragedy. They stripped it of its vague semi-specificity, buffing out the group's name and refinishing the onyx slabs. The group was pleased. It's not that they didn't want a memorial for their tragedy; they just wanted a good one. By the time I saw it, its name had been changed. It was no longer the city's *Memorial to the Group*, but an archetype of public art.

I looked at the sundial in the middle of the plaza. Over an hour had passed since I'd left for lunch. I needed to get back to my assemblages. But as I turned to the west, a wave of lethargy overtook me, and I stumbled over to one of the concrete slabs and sat. I felt suddenly exhausted—drained by the prospect of returning to that work. That was no mystery; it wasn't a stretch to imagine why I might not be motivated to fit pipes into bigger pipes. What I was surprised by was the apathy I felt, too, creeping through my mind like a parasite through an insect. The apathy was a true force, a heroic sensibility. I was deathly unafraid of consequence. Why? I didn't know. I didn't want to know. To know was to negate the metamorphosis. To return to fear.

There was a spirit in my exhaustion. I was sleepy and full of protein—and I didn't care about a thing.

I decided to keep walking east. The avenues kept appearing, one after the next, unnamed, with unnamed plazas at the intersections and unnamed workers taking breaks on sunny blocks of concrete. After the fourth or fifth plaza, I made a goal of reaching the end of the factory area. I wanted to gaze into the surrounding desert, feel a little alone. So I hoofed it. At some juncture, I stopped a fellow who was pacing back and forth in front of his factory. I asked him how much farther it was till I'd hit the desert. He pointed down the road in the direction I was walking. Then he took a map out of his pocket and gave it to me. I glanced at it to see if the city had changed and it seemed to have changed considerably, though I knew that wasn't likely.

Finally, the town stopped. I stepped into the sand beyond the end of the road, my brown leather shoes already dusty. The cuffs of my uniform, too. I opened my mouth and dust flitted around my teeth. It coated my tongue. I squinted into the distance and saw a black house—the same one I'd seen from the window of the bus. I couldn't stop now. I was getting exercise. Exploring some obsolete, retired civilization—the ruins of a bygone world. Ancient Roman or Greek or Chinese or Indian.

I arrived at the black house after a half hour of walk-ing across a shadowless stretch of rocky, barren terrain, waves of heat roiling in the air beneath an enormous sky of washed-out blue. The colors of everything were red, black, and blue, and the blue was shimmering. The house was made of wood, its wooden-slat siding running vertically from the dusty ground up to the dormer window above the door. I touched the scalding wood with my hands. A small house. I circled it. Only one window; only one door. The door was open.

A soft electric light dangled from the water-stained ceiling. There was a dirty twin cot on a brass frame in the corner. An old wooden wardrobe and an old wooden desk. A black telephone and a red telephone and papers on the old wooden desk. Black-framed glasses resting on an open scheduling book. A lamp with a flesh-colored shade. A forest-green officer's jacket draped on the chairback. Behind it, on the wall, a complex organizing system: a 12x14 grid, each column labeled *Zelle 1, Zelle 2, Zelle 3, Zelle 4, Zelle 5,* and so on. Paper cards were tacked on each square, with names written on them, and numbers. More filing cabinets behind the desk. A ring of iron keys hanging from a protruding nail.

An old radio stood on a rickety stool. I flicked it on. Big band swing. I sat down at the desk and pulled out the drawer. Odds and ends. Paperclips, stamps, envelopes, a knot of twine, rusted hardware, a Luger pistol, swastika cufflinks. I picked up the cufflinks and bounced them around in my palm, then placed them back in the drawer and closed it. They almost seemed real. The papers on the desk were elaborate architectural blueprints in laminated plastic. They smelled like cologne. Written on them were designs for hatches, chambers, cells, columns. After the song ended, the same song started up again, running in a loop. A bopping number: I could imagine the bandleader's swaying shoulder, his back hunched over his drum kit, his eyes closed, sweat on his forehead, a faint red ring around his neck from his too-tight collar. I swiveled in the chair and looked again at the organizing system. I couldn't read the names; they had been intentionally blurred to avoid specificity. I dragged the chair over to the front door and stood on it to look out of the window. Decals had been stuck on the glass to make it seem like there were other constructions out there—one was of a faraway gallows and the ground beneath them, rendered in a distancing perspective. Beyond that, across the desert, was the real factory town, housing my own Factory 7A.

I spun around on the chair and focused on my feelings. I was seriously discomfited by the...piece? Fabrication? Memorial? My inability to identify just what this *was*, that was precisely the thing that made me so uncomfortable with it. Nazi symbology was painful to see, as it always was when I discovered swastikas sprayed on park benches and bus stops at home. And the infinite iterations of SS insignia—too many to keep track of or even identify as such. It gave me chills. My ears pricked. The energy was bad. I didn't know how else to describe it. I focused on the energy. It was perfect—and wrong. It was the singular achievement of art: the transmission of feeling from artist to observer. It felt terrible to be in there, which was how I knew the piece succeeded, and how I knew it was artwork. The elements were fabricated; the feeling was uncanny. By reproducing whatever this was out in a contextless desert, it took on an ontological dimension, questioning its existence and by extension my own—and my complicity in the illusion.

I left the room and circled the property again. On the north-facing wall I spotted a square of text made faint by dust. I cleared it off with my cuff.

### Block Elf Aufseher Büro

Miriana Grannoff

Wood, glass, fiberglass, resin, paint, rubber, PVC pipe

Reproduction

A kommandant's office, as I suspected. This was a *dazzling* discovery. And unsurprisingly the work of Grannoff. I had such an urge to talk to her about it. This was architecture! I'd had no idea that Grannoff had this skill set, that she could fabricate a structure so authentic, so sophisticated. And now that I knew the piece was Grannoff's, I could push my analysis farther. It was clear now that *Block Elf Aufseher Büro* was a memorial, a resonant callback to a time of horror. Isolate the terror in the desert where it can't hurt anyone, but where it can be visited—as a reminder.

There was more language on the plaque, detailed plans for future expansion:

*Visitors will be able to examine the full-scale replica of a gas chamber door, built with hinges on the outside and a cage around its peephole to prevent victims from easily breaking it down. Also on view will be the gas column built to introduce Zyklon-B pellets.*

I was excited by Grannoff's vision. She wanted to aestheticize the banality of evil, to take something so ruthlessly bureaucratic and bronze it in memory—to resituate it in a violent context (the desert), to recreate it molecule by molecule (the knot of twine), and to show it in light (the isolation). Art becoming operative.

If I wasn't careful, I'd be in love with Grannoff by nightfall.

I dragged my foot through the sand next to the house. It parted under my shoe. The sun was beginning to set, and I realized that I had no way to tell the time. The thought of trudging back across the sand to reach the factory was unbearable. Besides, work was probably just about done for the day. And I didn't want to leave. I scanned the horizon—I was alone out here. It was glorious to be alone. To the west was where I'd come from. To the east, south, north—the steppe, nothing but rocks and sand. It was peaceful here.

I went around to the east side of the house and ran my hand along the wall, then knocked. The wood was sturdy. I couldn't see through to the interior through the slats. I could spend the night here, I thought; it wouldn't be too crazy. I'd be the first one back at work in the morning. If I got in trouble for abandoning my post, then being the first in would be the beginning of forgiveness. I wasn't hungry or thirsty. The more I thought about it, the more the thought appealed to me. I never did things like this back home. I'd never gone camping. I'd never spent the night beneath the stars. Some people would say that spending the night beneath the stars was a privilege. Camping seemed like a bourgeois luxury, a kind of simulated homelessness. "Roughing it" was what the working class did every day of their lives. This was a good way to show my solidarity.

I sat down on the floor inside, my back against the far wall. I rested my elbows on my knees and listened to the wind gently blowing outside. I was right: I couldn't feel a draft through the wood. The night would pass fine. I decided I'd help it pass with a little music. I liked that big band number from the radio. I went over to the radio and switched it on. It played through the swing number again, which I enjoyed, but instead of starting back up again, it started to purr static. Then a voice that I hadn't noticed before came on. It was a deep masculine voice, with a German accent. "The rotten bones are trembling," it said in English, followed by the sound of a needle scratching into a record groove. A children's choir began to sing in German. A marching song. I hated the sound of children's choirs, but I let them sing for the sake of stimulation, until the loop began again: "The rotten bones are trembling," the needle scratch, the choir. Probably a marching anthem for a youth movement. A clever gimmick from Grannoff. I switched off the radio and waited for the tube to cool down and the ruby light to fade to dark. Instead, the choir started up again. I wondered how old the recording was.

No—I wondered why it was still playing after I had killed the power. I lifted the radio off the stool and turned it around in my hands, a National Socialist Doppler Effect. There was no obvious place to get at its guts—no panel concealing batteries, no technical off switch. I sighed, then took the jacket off the chair and draped it over the radio. It muffled the children, which only made them sound ghostlier—not quiet.

Then I had an idea.

I rummaged through the desk drawer and pulled out the Luger. I passed the gun from one hand to the other, feeling its weight. I'd never held one before. The metal was freezing. These things were the end of everything. Nevertheless, I slid the chanting radio under my armpit and walked outside into the night desert and didn't stop walking until I was well away from the house. Stars blinked in the sky. It was clear enough to see swirling gold. I placed the radio down on a smooth rock and walked backwards several paces. I lifted the Luger and looked down the barrel at the radio. Victim becoming oppressor. "The rotten bones are trembling," it said. The kids began to sing their German.

I took a deep breath and exhaled slowly. Then I pulled the trigger.

A small blast jerked my arm into my chest and a piece of something sharp ripped my cheek. My ears rang. The radio smoldered on the rock. The German children warbled into silence. I touched my cheek and saw my blood by the light of the stars. A piece of the radio had grazed my skin, but it was only a surface wound.

Peace fell upon the kommandant's office. I resumed my place on the floor and covered my body with the officer's jacket. I shivered, my eyelids drooping. I doubted I could sleep that way, but I managed. I woke up some hours later with my head between my knees. It was still dark. I got up and stretched, walked around the office. The moon had risen and now hung a few inches above the horizon. It was waxing gibbous and the color of watery mustard. I walked over to the wall behind the desk and examined the organizing system, seeing if I could make out any of the names on the cards. The names were all blurred, but the shapes seemed specific: blurry shapes that took up the space of four or five-letter names, six or seven-letter surnames. I ran my finger down the cards, looking for two shapes that corresponded in size to my name. Why wouldn't my name be listed on a catalogue of prisoners in a Nazi jail? Some things just seemed inevitable. When I found one, I ran my fingers over the shapes, and they seemed to come into focus, as if I were wiping dust away from the letters. S— Zelnik. I tried to clarify the names on the other cards, but it seemed it was only mine that would resolve into focus. My eyes were deceiving me, I knew they were, but it was too difficult to convince myself that what I was seeing wasn't there. I slapped my cheek, forgetting the cut, and yelped in pain. I touched the cards on the board. I had what I could only call an intuition. A premonition. A whisper in the wind told me I would find the secret behind all things. I pressed each card until one of them clunked back into the wall, as if falling into place. Behind me, on the floor, a square of wood shot open, releasing a cloud of dust. I laughed. Somewhere in my subconscious I must have remembered that Grannoff liked these sorts of tricks, artworks doubling as adventure narratives.

I peered through the trap door. Darkness. A sound. A buzzing sound. It engulfed the kommandant's office and sent my hands to my ears. I longed for the German children instead. I stared deeper into the hole and, as my eyes adjusted to the darkness, began to detect a faint fluorescent yellow. It looked familiar to me. It *felt* familiar to me. It had the smell of a paperback exposed too long to the sun. Leaning closer, I placed a hand wrong and began to fall into the hole but was able to redirect my body at the last moment. I toppled awkwardly, jerking clear of the opening like a marionette. I rolled onto my stomach and looked down into the darkness, where the buzzing and the yellow were foulest. My pupils dilated. When yellow carpeting came into focus, I realized where I knew the sound and smell from—Grannoff's earlier work in the factory basement. There were carpeted tunnels beneath the artworks.

I could go down there, I thought.

I pulled myself into the fetal position and shut my eyes. I felt clouds in my mind. Stuffing in my mind. The buzzing was a hacksaw in the kommandant's office. The hacksaw said I should go down there. I put my back against the trapdoor and dug my heels into the wood. They kept slipping. Finally, I found traction, and pushed until the door closed. The buzzing stopped. I was supine over the trapdoor; I could feel it vibrating.

# SEVEN

**L** EAVING THE ARTWORK left me with an enormous sense of longing—as if torn away from the love of my life—and I walked heavily across the desert back into town. Workers were already arriving at their factories, but I walked against the stream and got on a bus back to Duma once the commuters had all filed out. I was hardly thinking about my placement, my assemblages; I was much too manic with excitement to sit on my stool and fidget with pipes.

When we got back to Duma, I hopped off the bus and headed to the housing area where Erich lived with his private garden. I couldn't remember which house was his, so I killed time with my hands in my pockets, kicking at the gravel on the path. People walked by occasionally and I smiled at them or averted my eyes. I didn't like loitering. Loitering felt criminal. I thought back to Erich telling me *you can do whatever you want here.* What I wanted to do was loiter and kick rocks. So that's what I did. But I couldn't kick the feeling that I was being judged for it.

Eventually, he appeared, sweaty from some kind of manual labor, a dark cat's face of perspiration on his white t-shirt. He had a hand towel wrapped around his neck. He was walking down the lane toward me but hadn't seen me yet. I watched him wipe the sweat from his forehead with the towel before I yelled his name.

"Zelnik, is that you?" he called.

"It's me!" I called back. I met him halfway and we shook hands in the shadow of a cypress tree.

"What brings you here?"

"I'm looking for Miriana. Do you know where she is?"

Erich seemed troubled for a moment. Then something snapped and he beamed at me. "Sure, sure," he said. "Let's talk over here." I followed him up the gravel path toward a cutaway in the trees that provided a bit of privacy. A single plastic chair, covered in tree gunk, sat in the clearing. He dragged it into the sun and sat while I stood. "What do you need to talk to her about?"

"I've just come from the desert!" I said.

Erich shot back in his chair. "You what?"

"The desert! Miriana's work out in the desert. The officer's büro. It was *incredible*," I said. I wasn't sure why he was so nonplussed. It was simple. "May I speak with her? I must speak with her about it."

"Hold on a minute, Zelnik," he said. "You were out there this early?"

"I spent the night there," I explained. Saying that seemed odd, but it felt true. "The way the sun hits it in the morning. Sunrise over the kommandant's office. It was breathtaking."

"You spent the *night*? You're crazy, man."

"I missed the bus back to town."

Erich laughed. "Crazy, man. You are not the Zelnik I remember."

"I'm some version of him," I said. What did Erich remember about me that I didn't?

Erich stood, the plastic creaking beneath him. "Have they not given you a placement yet?"

"They did. It's not right for me. It's nothing. I'll sort it out. Don't worry about it."

"Not right?"

"Well, it's a bit—"

"Beneath your station?"

"I didn't want to put it that way."

"That's all right," Erich said. "I'll put it that way for you." He turned his head to think. He had bumps on his scalp and chin. I could smell his musk.

"You know, I don't even know what you do here," I said.

"When you pulled in, did you drive past a really strange, glassy building, on a little lake? Kind of looked like a flower?"

"It was dark when we got in."

"You can't miss it. Next time you're out by the athletic complex, look for it. That's where I work. You'd have to be blind to miss it, Zelnik."

"I'll look for it."

"If I could get you a transfer, would you be interested?"

"Sure," I said. "I mean, yes."

"Would you be willing to do a favor for me in exchange for it?"

"It depends on the favor, I guess."

He must have interpreted this as bargaining. "If you help me, in addition to a transfer, I'll see if I can bump you up on the list to get one of these beauties," he said. He gestured at the houses with lush gardens. "I had to wait a long time to get mine."

"I thought you said you were here when they were built. I thought you just picked one and moved in."

"There's a high turnover," he said.

"Why?"

"You're in the Crescent, right? Someone in your building is manufacturing pamphlets. Behind one of your neighbors' doors there's a person with a printing operation. If you can find out who he is, you'll get your transfer."

This didn't explain what he meant by high turnover.

"What's wrong with making pamphlets?"

"They're inflammatory." Erich smiled at me, a real smile. "If you look around, you'll see one of them. He dumps them in the plaza sometimes. No one ever sees him. You probably have a pamphlet under your door right now."

"Huh."

"You'll do it?"

"I guess I can look around."

"Say, that's great." Erich shook my hand. His palm was like wet sandpaper against mine. He glanced behind him for a moment like he was expecting someone. "So you want to meet Miriana?"

"Yes," I said. "Yes."

"Grand. Come with me."

I followed Erich off of the shaded path and back toward his house.

"Zelnik, any luck finding your uncle?"

"None yet. Someone at the factory said they knew him."

"And did they?"

"I don't think so," I said. "I think she was confused."

We walked along in silence for a minute. I wondered if Erich would ring Miriana from his house phone, if he had one—or maybe Miriana lived in one of the neighboring houses.

"Well, let me know if there's anything I can do to help," he said in afterthought. He led me around his garden. I was going to take him up on the offer, but suddenly we were through the front door and standing in a foyer that gave way to a sunken living room. A wall of windows let in the blistering morning light. He pointed to a leather sectional sofa and I sat; then he disappeared around a corner, and I heard clanging. I looked at a generic land-scape painting that hung on the wall. I heard Erich say something but couldn't tell whether he was speaking to me or into the phone. I rose to my feet and was about to call to him when Miriana Grannoff walked into the room. She paused, startled, hand on her heart.

"Mr. Zelnik?" she said. "Is it really you?"

Heat flooded my cheeks. "I can't believe you

remember me," I said. I felt the chill of nervous sweat on the back of my neck.

Grannoff came forward, her red-and-gold yukata flowing behind her like a fishing net. She extended her hand—skeletal, freckled, fingers downturned and laden with rings—and I took it, my thumb closing over her knuckles. She looked at me and smiled, pale pink lips parting to reveal perfect teeth. She was the exact image of my memory, gracefully aged a decade, lines deeper on her face but all life force remaining.

"It's wonderful to see you, former student Zelnik," she said, using the formal mode of address. It was jarring to hear my home language spoken; Erich and I only conversed in English, per Duma's regulation.

She sat on the sofa next to me, crossed her legs. Her feet were bare. She stretched her toes and lit a cigarette. Erich came out of the kitchen carrying three drinks in a triangle between his pressed hands. Water glasses, ice tinkling.

"Hot out there," he said.

I sipped from the proffered glass; it was not water. It burned on the way down. I turned red as Erich sat in an armchair near Grannoff. They looked at each other and laughed. I dissociated.

"Zelnik agreed to help me find the pamphleteer," said Erich.

Grannoff gave me a long, approving nod. "That's fabulous, former student Zelnik. We're proud of you."

I took another sip. The melting ice had turned the drink milky white.

"A gift from the brass," said Erich, holding his glass up to the light. It split into three rays on the far wall.

"Oh, hold that, Erich. Let me get my camera." Grannoff put a hand on my knee and hoisted herself up. She ran off into the hallway, her feet making a pleasant shuffling sound.

"Hurry. My arm's getting tired."

"Shut up," she said, returning. She had a self-developing film camera cradled in one hand; in the other her drink sloshed over the side of its glass. I held the glass for her while she crouched by Erich's knees and framed the shot, the camera at an angle. She took a shot, removed the printed photograph, then took another. Then she put them on the counter to develop.

I watched Erich watching Grannoff while this scene transpired. His bottom lip was trapped between his teeth. She rested her arm over his knees while she flapped a photograph back and forth. When she had taken enough for her liking, she gathered them in a stack and returned to her seat next to me.

"No good. No good. No good," she said, chucking the photos one by one across the living room. One was decent. She handed it to me. She had managed to capture the refraction of Erich's glass in such a way that the light was unidentifiable as light; instead, I saw three nearly perpendicular beams, like the wires of a suspension bridge against a pitch-black sky.

"It's wonderful, Professor Grannoff."

"You must call me Miriana."

"I will," I tried to hand it back to her.

"Keep it. You really think so?"

"Yes," I said. "Thank you." I put it carefully in my pocket.

"A gift from me to you."

"Thank you."

I was aware of the clipped way I was speaking. I was embarrassed by it but, paradoxically, I didn't care. I felt at ease—I felt I could do anything in the company of these friends. I began to lose track of myself in my mind's eye. I was aware of an awareness that I was impressionable—and aware that I couldn't do anything about it. The urge to speak with Miriana about her work hadn't abated, though I didn't want to offend her by changing the subject. I wanted to impress her so badly.

Erich shifted in his chair, cast a leg over the armrest. "Tell her where you've come from, Zelnik."

Miriana raised an eyebrow. "Yes, tell us."

"Watch her expression when you do, Zelnik. Don't miss it."

"Where, darling?"

"The desert," I said. "Your piece in the desert. The kommandant's office."

"Tell her what you did there," said Erich.

"I spent the night there," I said. "I slept on the floor."

Miriana's face did indeed do something extraordinary. Her eyes widened twofold; her ears pulled back; her jaw fell open. I saw where the base of her tongue plunged down into her throat. At last, her hand found the lapels of her robe. She tossed them open, revealing her freckled clavicle.

"It's so hot," she said, fanning herself with her hand. The way she shifted so abruptly from the conversation made me think it had ended. But it hadn't. "Zelnik—why on Earth?"

This was my cue. "Professor Grannoff. Miriana. It was an honor to have seen your work. After you left Barnova, a cohort of your supporters spearheaded a letter-writing campaign that generated over one thousand letters. We picketed outside of President Stankov's office until the police shot at us. Many of us were expelled. When we learned that you had emigrated, we were, with respect, distraught. The movement died. Some of my class-mates—I don't know what happened to them." I took a sip of my drink. "And now, to find you here, to see your work—well, to see what you have been doing, the memorials, the monument. I understood. You needed to emigrate."

"And the work?"

"It's the best you've ever done."

"The house? You love it that much?"

"And the lamps."

Miriana looked at Erich. "He saw the lamps?"

"Zelnik sees everything," said Erich.

"And you thought the office was brilliant?"

"Brilliant isn't a strong enough word," I said. "To recontextualize a place as banal and terrible as that office. To put it in the middle of the desert. You took a site of horror and, displacing it, turned it into a monument. There's a real mastery in it. All of a sudden I was back at the Architectural Institute, studying the works of the masters." I sighed in awe. "How did you stumble onto that idea? When did you learn to fabricate like that? In South America?"

"Yes, in Buenos Aires I met a group of German expats, in the suburbs. I learned a lot from them," Miriana said. She placed her finger and thumb on either side of her right eye, then pried the lids apart. She leaned in close, her pupil shrinking, iris roaming; she drank in my face as I examined the fractal blood vessels in the white. She leaned back. "I met Erich there," she said. She kited her hand in his direction and he took it by the fingers.

"Hello, dear," he said languidly. She was twenty, twenty-five years his senior.

"Hello, dear," said Miriana.

"I moved to Argentina after graduation. The best decision I ever made."

Miriana extinguished her cigarette in her nearly full drink. Then she took my hand and turned to me. "Hello, dear," she said. Her hand was soft and warm, and I was overcome by how few strange hands had touched mine in my life. "I'm touched you like it, dear," she said. "I am proud of that work—but you have not yet seen my very best work." The three of us were connected, with Miriana as conduit. I felt an energy flow out of me and into her—but when I saw it pass through her chest, out of her arm, and toward Erich, I pulled my hand away. The serenity I'd been feeling dried up. Miriana and—*Erich?*

"Hm," she said.

I looked at my glass, sweating invitingly on the table. I was thirsty. Erich stood before I could reach for it.

"We've got things to do, don't we?" he said. He helped me to my feet.

Miriana kissed me on the cheek and ear. "Find the pamphleteer," she said. "The art is trifling." She disappeared into the hallway, her yukata billowing behind her. There was still so much I wanted to say to her. I turned to Erich in desperation.

"Can I see her again?"

He led me to the door. I was outside before I regained myself. I walked away from Erich's as if I'd been wound up and released.

"Good luck," he called out.

I volleyed back that I wouldn't need it.

# EIGHT

ERICH WAS RIGHT. A pamphlet was waiting for me on the floor as soon as I walked into my apartment. There was also a rancid smell. I looked around and saw that the refrigerator had been left open and the interior yellow light had burned out. The fruit had spoiled, and fruit flies drifted like dust motes around the open door.

I threw the squishy brown fruit out and shooed away the fruit flies and opened the window to air out the apartment. I was half-starved; I hadn't eaten since lunch the day before. Fortunately, there was still a packet of vacuum-sealed synthetic meat in the drawer that seemed immune to spoilage.

I sat at the kitchen counter, peeled the plastic off the meat, and fed myself one slice at a time. I felt better once I'd consumed the last morsel. I felt like myself.

The pamphlet was a typical tri-fold affair with images printed on each of the six sides. The stock was flimsy. Three of the pamphlet's faces depicted Rorschach blots that reminded me of my parents, a train depot, and a ceremonial urn in the Second Empire style that I somehow knew was filled with ashes. Two more showed identical images of a felt suit dangling off a wall. I recognized the felt as similar to the rolls of carpet that lined the walls of the photograph I kept in my nightstand. I retrieved the photograph and compared the material: it seemed to be the same, in fact. The final image in the pamphlet appeared to be a blown-up detail of craquelure on an oil-coated canvas, resembling a network of firing neurons or an aerial photograph of dried riverbeds.

Something else occurred to me. I got the photograph that Miriana had taken of the refracted light and held it next to the photograph I'd found in the credenza. Both photographs had been printed on the same self-developing stock—indeed, measured the same dimensions, too. I wondered if the one from the credenza was also Miriana's work. If so—why had it wound up in my living room furniture?

I spent a half-hour studying the pamphlet. I had decided that I would not return to Factory 7A if I could help it, and that was driving my motivation to fulfill the favor asked of me by Erich. The faster I completed my mission, the faster I could get a transfer to a more fitting position—and the faster I did all that, the less likely it was that I'd get in trouble for abandoning my post. For the life of me, though, I could not find anything "inflammatory" about the pamphlet. This was not at all like the texts Erich and I had studied in Hallen's class. If anything, it was most like the stuff I studied in my art history lectures. Better yet, the stuff students copied cheaply at the paper store and handed out at parties to perform their eccentricities.

The truth was, I quite liked the pamphlet. It was much nicer than any of the student work I had seen at Barnova. Where was the polemic? I saw no message. Those student pamphlets always had text. Quotes from Marx or Yudekhezko or Namboodiripad or Yohanofski. No text here. No clues as to authorship. Functionless art. Did that make it "trifling," as Miriana had called it? Still, I liked it.

A fingernail of sun appeared outside my window. I sat on one of the cushier bits of modular furniture and examined the light through the open window. It had the pale, yellowish color of a zested lemon rind. The grass was parched, stiff, brown. The hill was patchy. I swiveled on the cushion and took in my apartment, my home for the last few—weeks? months? It was hard to say. I added *buy a calendar* to the To-Do List I kept in my mind. Also on the list: *eat more greens.* I needed to buy a duster, too. There was dust everywhere, a skin of it on every surface. I added *duster* to my list. I stood to swipe my hand along the top of the cupboard—it came back gray—and as I did, I caught a whiff of myself. I hadn't showered for two days.

I took a shower, and when I got out, night had fallen, which seemed strange. Hadn't it just been lunchtime? I dressed, then exited my apartment into the Crescent's curving hallway. I needed to find my uncle. That should have been my priority the whole day. I'd gotten distracted, pulled away from what was really important. Not this business with the pamphlets, or my work assignment. I looked down the hall to the right: nothing. I looked to the left: nothing. I chose left and immediately paused before my next-door neighbor's entryway. I'd go door-to-door. I counted backwards from three and then I knocked.

The woman who appeared in the crack had soft, delicate features that were charmingly smushed onto her face. She had narrow, anxious eyes and a downturned nose, and her skin was covered in freckles that spread across her nose like pebbles on a white shore.

"You're not holding anything," she said.

I looked down at my hands.

"Come in anyway." She grabbed my elbow and tugged me inside. Then she bolted the door. She came around and stood in front of me, scanning. She wore a black turtleneck despite the heat, and green corduroy pants. Her thick and curly dark hair was mostly caught in her sweater, giving her a compressed look. She had the poise of a spokesperson. Work boots on her feet. She might have been from my part of the world.

"So if you don't have the toner," she said, "then where is it?"

"I'm your neighbor. Zelnik." I stuck out my hand. It withered in the air untouched.

"I was expecting toner." She became maudlin and sat down on a bit of cushiony modular furniture identical to the one I had just been sitting on in my apartment, not fifty feet away.

Indeed, her apartment was exactly like mine, only more lived-in. She'd obviously been in the Crescent much longer than I had. There was art on the walls—the walls were covered with the stuff: lithographs, paintings, photographs, collages, magazine clippings. Old woodcuttings of geishas on bridges overlooking ponds. Portraits of regal-looking individuals before abstract purplish backdrops. A sculpture of a Roman statesman with its eyes gouged out standing on a pedestal. Empty fruit baskets hung from the ceiling above her sink. Her refrigerator lacked a handle. Her sink lacked a faucet. Her apartment was completely dilapidated. Her furniture was full of gashes and scuffs, was missing wheels, had lopsided legs. The state of things revealed the cheapness of the material.

I realized she was sniffling. I went to the kitchenette and found a glass clouded with water stains. A hole in the faucetless sink vomited water. I filled the glass and brought it to her. She took several gulps, then looked up at me through her dark rings of hair, sagging twisted on the cushion like a tender gargoyle. One of her ankles was folded behind the other, and one of her trouser cuffs tucked into a wool sock. It was clear to me that she had poor circulation. She turned her face up at me.

"You want something to *drink* drink?"

"Sure," I said, then realized why her voice had sounded familiar. Now that she had relaxed, and the disappointment of my lack of toner had worn off, her voice became what it usually was at rest: quiet, limpid, without cracks or static or phlegm. Her accent reminded me of home. I had eavesdropped on her through the wall, listened to her rendezvous with a man. She walked into her bedroom and drew the curtain for a moment, then emerged a moment later with two tumblers full of clear liquid. As the curtain fell back in place behind her, I glimpsed something boxy and metal with a big, attached lever.

She handed me a glass and I sniffed it. It was vodka—sort of.

I asked if she'd gotten it from the brass.

"The what? I made it myself."

It was awful.

"Who sent you—Zelnik? I don't know him," she said.

"No, *I'm* Zelnik," I said. I put my hand out again for a formal introduction. She looked at it and laughed.

"My neighbor, so you said," she said. "And you don't have my toner."

"I don't know what that is."

"Mm-hm." She had gray-blue eyes that sharpened at me. "Prove that you're my neighbor."

She unlocked her door and looked into the hallway before letting me out behind her. We walked ten paces to the right. I unlocked my door and pushed it open for her to enter.

"You first," she said. I entered. She followed. We stood in my living area, a cleaner and barer version of hers. "It doesn't look like you live here," she said.

She was right. There was very little in my apartment that suggested human habitation. It occurred to me to show her my valise, so I did. There were still some clothes in it. And then, for some reason, I wanted to show her the photograph I'd found in the credenza. She brought it up to her face.

"Don't show anyone else this picture," she said, handing it back to me. "Put it back where you found it. It doesn't matter."

"What doesn't matter?"

"Put it back in the credenza."

"For God's sake, what's your name?" I nearly shouted. She took a step back, inching toward my door. She was frightened and dark, like something shaking in the bushes.

"We'll talk in my apartment."

We reversed our tracks. An onlooker would find our movements intimately plotted, a silly dance routine. She poured us another round of her moonshine, and we sat on her ruined furniture. After drinking, she relaxed again at last, melting back into the wall. She pulled her hair out of her collar and tied it in a sloppy bun on top of her head. I could see her whole face now. It was a very Jewish face. Her lips curved downwards, and her eyebrows were thick and angry. The color of the skin beneath her eyes was dark blue. She clearly belonged to a generation of people who'd spent their lives boarding trains to frightening places.

"Margarette Khvalsky," she said. She held my gaze for a moment and smiled. "What is your first name, Zelnik?"

"I won't say."

"Wise," said Margarette. "When you came to my door, you didn't see anyone out there?"

"I never see anyone."

"Why did you knock on my door?"

I took the pamphlet out of my pocket and unfolded it.

"I'm looking for the person who makes these," I said. She took it from me and looked at it, then handed it back.

"I make them," she said. She rose from the cushion and drew the curtain back from the bedroom area. The big metal thing I'd seen earlier revealed itself to be a small printing press, jammed in the crevice between the bed and the wall. There were grease and ink stains all over the metal. I couldn't believe Erich's mission had turned out so easy to accomplish. That was it. I had accomplished it. Mission accomplished. I could get a house, a better job. If I was that kind of person. Was I that kind of person?

My gaze fell on her bed, where a knotted sheet revealed a restless night. After she decided I'd looked enough, Margarete closed the curtain. "Tell me the truth," she said. "Were you sent by someone?"

"Yes."

There didn't seem to be any point in lying about it. I wasn't afraid of Margarette. She could not hurt me.

I watched her light a cigarette, gather her lips into the corner of her mouth, and exhale her smoke in a tube like someone accustomed to a difficult life.

"So you will tell them about me," she said. It wasn't a question.

"No," I said.

She held her cigarette by her face, her elbow resting on her knee, her back hunched. Her gaze was fixed on the floor by my feet.

"I am looking for my uncle," I said. I described his features, which, as always when I did this, manifested an image of him in my mind that was just a collection of floating, unconnected body parts in a vat of plasmatic liquid. "Does it ring a bell?"

Without taking her eyes from the floor, Margarette said, "You'll never see him again."

"You know him?"

"It doesn't matter."

My heart began to pump faster. "So you know him," I said. "Tell me where he is. Please. I won't report you."

She looked at me now, drew on her cigarette, then smirked. "You crack so easily."

This accusation triggered some defensiveness in me. I could feel it bubble up from the recesses, scolding me for forgetting my mission. My mission. To win approval. To be approved. I heard Miriana's voice; I heard Erich's. Their voices ran lines like dissonant saxophones playing against each other, and yet the overall sound was pleasing in its disharmony.

"Are you all right?"

I opened my eyes. Margarette was crouched in front of me, holding a glass of water. She handed it to me, pushed it gently towards my mouth. I drank.

"I came to Duma with my sister Sarah. Where is Sarah? Where did she go?" Margarette asked.

"I don't know," I said. "I'm sorry."

"I don't know where your uncle is."

"I'm not going to report you," I said.

"Thank you." Margarette returned to her seat. She exhaled, then took off her sweater; her shirt clung to the fuzzy fabric and rose; for a brief moment I saw the extreme contours of her ribcage. She wasn't just skinny—she was emaciated.

She caught me staring.

"You need to stop eating the food in your refrigerator. It's in your face. You go slack. Your cheeks drop. They are poisoning you. Stop eating their food."

I wanted to laugh but caught myself. This sounded like the paranoid ravings of a woman with a totally circumscribed life, a woman with no ability to see beyond the reach of her own arms. Though delusions like this were understandable when your life was just one loss after another. She was groping blindly for explanation. I felt sad for her.

Margarette put her face into her hands. Her bun bobbed at me. To change the subject, I asked her where she was from.

Her response was muffled. She took her face out of her hands and repeated it. "I won't tell you," she said. Then she smiled for the first time.

"You don't want me vacationing there."

"There are no tourists where I'm from."

"Me neither," I said. She looked at me with, I thought, a face of recognition. We were speaking English, but her accent was very similar to mine. "I heard you through the wall one night," I said. "You were with a man. I didn't hear anything bad. I don't mean to scare you. I just wanted to come clean. So we could be equal."

"Equal? What does that even mean, *equal?*"

"On common ground."

"We're beneath the ground." She reached over to the sill to collect a pad and a pen. She jotted something down, then ripped it from the pad.

"Have you been to the grain elevators?" she asked.

I shook my head.

"Hm." She held my gaze for a few moments. I couldn't read the expression. I felt ashamed that I hadn't been wherever, why-ever. She handed me the paper she'd torn.

"That's his number," she said. "For not telling them about me. For when you need a break from this life."

"Whose?"

"The man you heard me with." Margarette stood up, then pulled me to my feet. She pushed me to the door. "I hope you find your uncle," she said. I bowed dumbly as her door closed in my face.

In the hallway, I wondered what I would tell Erich. It seemed inescapable to me that I would have to report to him, to tell him that I had—or hadn't—found the pamphleteer. As would Miriana, I imagined. She seemed to have a stake in this, whatever it was exactly. Competition, maybe. A rivalry. Perhaps she disliked that Margarette was playing outside of the rules. But that didn't ring true for the Miriana Grannoff I knew. Nevertheless, I would have to answer for my task if I wanted to see her again. And I did, desperately.

One thing was now certain, though: I did not want to snitch on Margarette. She had gone through enough.

I returned to my apartment and gave it a thorough dusting. I began in the kitchenette, then took on the bedroom, and ended in the living area, where with a wetted cloth I attacked the window, scrubbing the film away from the glass. It came off like potato skin that had been scorched onto the surface of a skillet. In some places the skin was so heavy and stubborn I had to use a wooden spoon I found under the sink. I chiseled away, trying to be careful not to scratch the glass. But even when I managed to carve out a satisfying chunk of it, there was yet another layer of dead skin beneath. I pried a crumb of it off the glass and rolled it between my thumb and index finger. It gave, like rubber cement. I flicked it back at the glass and it stuck.

After working on that for a while, I picked up the piece of paper that Margarette had given me. I stared at it for a while before realizing what the problem was: I didn't have a phone. I hadn't seen a phone anywhere. I went back over to Margarette's apartment and knocked on the door again. She was wearing a different outfit when she answered. A work uniform, a gray utility jumpsuit with a significant brown belt at the waist. Her hair was gathered in a ponytail and she wore black leather gloves.

"I don't have a phone," I said.

She looked at the paper for a moment, then said, "What time do you want him to come?"

"Any time after dark, I suppose. You have a phone?"

"I'll let him know."

"Can I use your phone to call my uncle?" I said.

"What's his number?"

"I don't know."

"That's what I thought," she said, and closed the door in my face.

I went back to my apartment, where daylight now shone in broadly, and sat around until it returned to darkness. As I waited for my guest to arrive, I took a shower and tidied; the place was a mess all over again. At least the gunk on my windows had cleared itself up. I wondered if it was a kind of bacteria activated by sunlight, or humidity. Tidying made me feel better, as did knowing that company was expected. I enjoyed playing the host from time to time. I wished I had some of Margarette's moonshine. I was feeling unexpectedly nervous.

There was a knock on the door. It was Kamwendo.

"Resnick, is that you?" he said.

"It's Zelnik."

"Right. Sorry."

"Kamwendo."

"Winger, actually." He smiled charmingly. His teeth were straight and small but his mouth was large and fleshy and his lips full and purple.

I let him in. His shoulder grazed my chest and I smelled oranges. He took a few steps into the living area and stood, looking around. He put one of his hands in his pocket while the other swung by his side. He turned and looked at me. He was wearing form-hugging navy trousers and a navy dress shirt. Outside of that was a sharp red cardigan that made him seem like an athlete on his evening off. He looked virtuous.

"It's truly uncanny," he said. "You truly do look exactly like Resnick." He may have misinterpreted the perplexity on my face, because he added, "That's not a bad thing."

"I thought you worked at the pier," I said.

"I do both."

"Yes, but *why?*"

He had a sharp Adam's apple that bobbed when he laughed. "For the *favors*," he said.

"I've heard about these favors," I said. I poured him a glass of water and he drank it quickly. He had thick, cropped hair that grew in a half-halo around his head, and slightly reddish eyes. He was tired, I imagined. "What do your favors get you? And don't say 'this and that.'"

He smiled. That row of teeth. "You're my last of the night," he said.

Winger placed the glass on the credenza and turned to me. I took him by the hand into my bed nook and asked him to take off his shoes, which he did, sitting on the edge of the bed, carefully unlacing. I crawled onto the bed behind him and wrapped my legs around his. He had a strong but pudgy midsection that I felt through his sweater and shirt. He leaned his head back against my collarbone and our cheeks touched. He was freshly shaven; I was not. He rubbed his face gently against mine and we listened to the bristles of my beard tick back and forth along his skin. I smelled the oranges more strongly, and something else, too, something old and fragrant like mothballs or formaldehyde. He leaned forward and wiggled out of his cardigan and shirt so I could better grasp his chest. There was a cluster of dark wiry hairs that I threaded my fingers through. He felt cold in my hands so I hugged him tighter to me. Eventually, we got out of our clothes and got under the covers. I didn't know how this was supposed to work—if I needed to be upfront with my selection of service, or what the selections even were; I didn't want to ask for a menu. We kissed for a while before he turned me over, which was exactly what I had hoped for. Afterward I placed a pillow over my head and cried uncontrollably for several minutes. I was half-conscious of his presence next to me while I was crying, half-conscious of the gratitude and relief I was feeling that he wasn't searching for his clothes while I sobbed. He didn't try to console me.

"Do you really work at the pier?" I asked him once I'd calmed down. The fact that he was still with me made me think he might spend the night. I very much wanted him to.

He faced me, our noses an inch apart on my lone pillow. He had a forest of short fine black hairs that clung to his bottom lip which I hadn't noticed before. I ran my thumb across them.

"Yes, I really work at the pier. Why don't you believe me?"

"Having a hard time believing we're near the ocean."

"You have no idea where you are."

I looked at the ceiling, the mildew. There were drooping sacs of trapped water and little shadowy fissures.

"You know Margarette," I said.

"You got my number from her," he said. "She's nice."

"I'm supposed to tell someone about her pamphlets."

"I don't want to know," said Winger. He moved his arm so I could be cradled. I wondered what all of this would cost me, one way or the other.

"You're from England, aren't you?" I asked.

He pulled back to look at me, mock surprise on his soft face.

"Naughty boy." He taunted me with his finger. "Asking the naughty questions."

"But you must be."

His eyes hardened. "You shouldn't ask. It'll only compromise you to know."

I looked away but there was nothing else to look at. The window was in the living room. "There are enormous distances between people here," I said.

"It's design. We're a 'global community,' aren't we?" This made me think of my uncle. I began to describe him to Winger, but he cut me off.

"I don't know him."

"You might."

"A Jew like you. I don't know him."

I felt my face and neck turn red. "Well, you look exactly like the horrible man who gave me my job."

"Don't be racist," said Winger.

I smacked him in the abdomen, and he curled like a snail's shell and then looked exhausted, his face drained of sheen, his eyes narrow. I imagined that in a previous life he ran a small, successful business, perhaps wine, or was the president of a union of bricklayers, a hereditary vocation, or a fine and inspiring schoolteacher. He kept curling until his knees were in his chest and he was on his side, lightly snoring.

Sometimes, at night, before I fell asleep, I would think about the paintings I would make if I were a painter. I had so many stills in my head. If I had been trained as a painter, I could extract them from my head and put them somewhere else. I could send them to my uncle to show him who I really was.

If I could paint, I would paint a door made of rich and grainy mahogany surrounded by acrid, smoking rubble—a painting that makes you think: how did the whole building burn but not the door? And what makes a door, anyway? Is it simply that which you can pass through, from one empty space to another, even if you can walk around it? Or must the door provide the only access to what it keeps on the other side? These are a few of the objectivist questions I would have this painting pose. Uncle, you would of course recognize this door as the one that my mother and father were trapped behind, in front of which stood a barricade of gendarmes. You held my hand as we watched from across the courtyard. It was the last time you did that. I never expected you to be a father to me when your brother died, but I did hope that you would be kind. I still don't understand why you weren't.

The image ended there. I tried to sleep. Naturally, I couldn't. I worried that a sac of ceiling would puncture and drench us in putrid water. I worried about the microbial universe. I worried about walking through a cloud of invisible, odorless, poisonous gas. I worried about getting shot with a gun. I envisaged holding a pistol in my hand and following the weight of it through my fist holding it and downward into the ground and into Earth, passing through the dirt and crust until I was jammed inside the solidity of Earth like an ancient, compressed mineral.

# A BRUTAL DESIGN

I listened to Winger breathing beside me. His chest rose and fell, much, I assumed, like the water by the pier where he worked. I would visit him there soon. I'd never lived by the ocean. Occasionally, I had lived by lakes. Barnova was near a freshwater reservoir that supplied the city. Ancient pines towered above it like sentries. When we met in the basement of some utility building—for what? the student newspaper?—the water seeped in through the floor, up through the sodden pastel yellow carpet. The room was stuffy and humid, shadowy. Boxy columns supported the concrete waffle ceiling. The walls were solid gray concrete. One long row of fluorescent lighting flickered intermittently and buzzed. The sodden yellow carpet. Parallel lines running through my life. The stacks were comprised of long tan metal carts on wheels, full of obsolete works of reference, or damaged, outdated, or recalled materials. A broad community desk, surrounded by chairs. Old and broken instrumentation. An inky and moldy aroma. Something behind my ear: the nub of a blue editor's pencil. A gray rat hacking away at a stack of papers, a cube of wet pulp. Hacking, gnawing it to bits.

Our group reserved the basement because no one went down there. I entered this memory at a moment when Zofia Percik and Obren Vučić were in a heated argument about Hallen. Obren had convinced Professor Hallen to agree to an anonymous interview for our paper. Zofia had been in Hallen's class with me. She knew him as a monster, and I agreed with her. I had learned that good people could periodically behave badly, but not *that* badly—that's how you knew who was *really* bad. Obren thought Hallen's scholarship was enough to prove his anti-partisan ethos, never mind his unorthodox pedagogy. Plenty of professors were eccentrics. Having a Barnova professor on record would be a coup for our paper, proving that the faculty weren't all toadies and milquetoasts. Like Professor Grannoff, some faculty members were holding on. Hallen taught an anti-Fascist literature course, Obren argued, wasn't that proof enough? Zofia said that just because you taught fascist literature didn't mean you were automatically repudiating it. Hadn't it been the deans who made it a prerequisite for graduating?

Subterfuge, said Zofia.

But did it really happen like that? Now I remembered a high window with a view of passing feet, their owners unaware of our presence in the nondescript basement. But we wouldn't have met in a windowed room, where we could be seen by the public. Would we?

The argument resolved itself abruptly when Obren reported that Hallen was already en route. Obren had prepared for the interview. He took masks out of his rucksack and passed them out. There were six of us, or seven, or eight. We all wrote articles, screeds, essays, manifestos. Obren asked me to transcribe. The masks were woolen and itchy; he had cut the eye holes out himself, for our safety and for Hallen's. This way everyone could be plausibly anonymous in the event that police pressed us for names at a later, inevitable date. Zofia looked at me with sullen eyes. She was very thin and her eyes were sapphire medallions set above cut cheekbones.

I wished I knew what I remembered. I thought that I remembered being in love. That we were in love. But maybe I just think that because of what happened next. I looked at Winger now, still snoring charmingly, a charming sleeper. A hard and soft body, accommodating, full of pleasure. The whiskers beneath his lip.

Obren had told Hallen to knock in a specific rhythm. We couldn't lock the door—the locks had been removed from all the doors on campus and all the residences where we slept on pallets, without pillows, prohibited from leaving our rooms after six in the evening.

Then: knuckles rapping at the door. The wrong pattern. Obren checked his wristwatch.

We had a chair jammed beneath the doorknob. Obren turned to look at us. His shoulders were up by his jaw as if he were sinking into himself. The knuckles rapped again—and then the door shattered open. A hole appeared in the back of Obren's skull and I tasted his mind in my mouth. The room filled with the stench of sulfur and little shouts of fire. Zofia was thrown against the wall and slid down it, leaving a painting of blood on the concrete.

Winger coughed in his sleep. I rubbed the broad plain of his back. He was radiating heat. It was dawn. I wasn't sure I had slept at all.

"Did you have any dreams?" I asked.

He moaned. "No one wants to hear about that."

"I do."

"Don't be sentimental." He pushed my arm away, rose, and dressed. I listened to him fill a glass with water from the faucet and drink it down. He moved back and forth across the living space, looking for something.

"Have you been to the grain elevators?" I asked.

He stopped pacing and looked at me. "No. Why?"

"Something Margarette said."

"Hm."

"Can I arrange for you to come back tonight?"

His eyes grew mean. He resumed his search. Eventually he found what he was looking for, his bag, and extracted a velvet pouch. He wagged it at me. "Coffee," he said, and tossed it onto the counter.

"You'll have some?"

"I've got to go," he said. His affect was restrained, businesslike. His hand was already around the doorknob.

"What about the favor I owe you?" I asked.

"I'll be in touch."

I got out of bed and wrapped the sheet around my waist. I was embarrassed. He glanced over his shoulder at my body and smirked rudely, then went out.

"Bye," I said.

I stared for a moment at the closed door, then dressed and made myself a cup of Winger's coffee with the tepid faucet water, then sat and stared out at the hill in the back. A patch of grass was illuminated. I looked at it intently until my vision began to blur and the yellow-green palette began to wiggle and squirm. I thought of the worms beneath the earth.

# NINE

I WAS PROBABLY EXPECTED at Factory 7A, but I couldn't bring myself to catch the bus. A part of me wanted to test the theory that work was voluntary; a part of me sought to be punished. I walked outside into another torment of heat and dust. I held my palm upward to feel the sun on my skin. No clouds in the sky. Heat glare above the dirt. The rich greens of the cypress trees burst against browns and tans. The air thrummed. I swatted at a fly and decided to study the architecture around Duma a bit. To see if I could offer any suggestions, come up with any ideas. I climbed the hill in the back of the Crescent. Each step kicked dust up into my mouth and eyes. At the top of the hill I could see an expanse of Duma. Sweat was already pin-pricking through my shirt. I could see Beau Gino Plaza and the houses with gardens where Erich lived. A headache mushroomed inside my skull. I massaged my temples and worked my jaw back and forth, hoping to release the pressure. There was no escape from the sun.

The roof of the Crescent served as a pathway from one elevated section of Duma to another, and along the pathway were glass viewing bubbles, half-spheres, built into the roof. A few people were walking up there, walking around the viewing bubbles as if they weren't even there. I hiked along the crest of the hill until it met the roof of the building, and then I walked along the path until I crossed one of the glass domes. The bubbles looked down into the hallways of the Crescent, illuminating sections about three feet in diameter. I caught sight of someone's head as it passed through the circle of light.

I walked until I reached the edge of the Crescent, then looked west to track a group of schoolchildren as they were led by teachers toward their school. The children were arranged in two long, neat columns—one for boys, the other for girls—and each column was headed by a teacher of the corresponding gender. The children wore uniforms: pleated blue skirts and white collared shirts for the girls; pleated blue trousers and white collared shirts for the boys. The shirts were tucked in. They passed beneath where I was standing to a diamond-shaped lot in a small valley between featureless slopes. The leaders held both front doors of the schoolhouse open while the children filed inside. It was a flat, single-story building with tall oval windows cut into the tan stone. Along its perimeter there was a continuous metallic brise-soleil through which the sun shone in blocky geometrics; the shadows made it appear as if the children were being grated as they entered.

I was touched by the specificity of the architecture. There were simply so many unique considerations that all coalesced into a unified personality. Each building was a variation on a theme. Virtually none featured an angle more acute or obtuse than ninety degrees. The Crescent aside, Duma was a settlement of straight, rational lines, uniform trajectories, soft light. Orderly. Perfect, in some respects—oppressively perfect. I thought about how modernism and totalitarianism were two sides of the same coin: these are buildings; beautiful buildings, aimed at making the worker more efficient and, resultantly, the human inside the worker happier, calmer, placated. The architect behind these buildings had a vision for a universe of unadulterated equality among all peoples.

I admired the idea that Duma's resident architect was thinking about the "greater good." Duma was a testing ground for ideologies. Whoever was Chief Architect had decided that this kind of modernist architecture would create a milieu most favorable for ideological explorations.

*You can do whatever you want here.*

The architecture was the result of Duma's Chief Architect doing whatever he wanted. Why he should choose such uniform building was anyone's guess. Maybe doing whatever he wanted was too much for him. People crave restrictions, guidelines, regulations—order. Though I was often awed by the architecture, I still wondered about the Chief Architect's evident feeling that chaos couldn't be beautiful, that cities built around desire lines couldn't work, that haphazardly built settlements needed to be organized and cleansed of irregularities. Maybe, I thought, if there was a lie to Duma, it would be most nakedly evident in its architecture.

I walked around lost in thought for a while longer, thinking that a settlement as methodical and neat as Duma really ought to have a directory where I could look up my uncle.

Then I began to feel sick.

It was an unusual feeling, not typical symptoms like nausea or a sore throat. My glands weren't enlarged. I didn't feel feverish. I sat down on a bench in the square and assessed my body. I was hot, yes, but I wasn't dehydrated. The sickness was in my mind.

I put my head in my hands for a few minutes, which helped more than I thought it would. When I looked up again, I spotted Miriana exiting a storefront and walking with purpose down a side street. Mesmerized, I followed at a distance, entranced by the shuffle of her black boots on the gravel path. She carried her head tilted upward and she swung her bag back and forth by her knees, like a dawdling schoolgirl. The back swished; the gravel crunched. Her boots rose and fell. Creases behind her knees. I watched them.

I felt myself losing control of myself. At one point, Miriana glanced over her shoulder at me and smiled, her eyes aslant, long hair whipped by the wind. The air around her head was a scramble of liquid colors. I followed her with tunnel vision. I had seen the film in which this scene played, as we crested a hill and beheld the settlement, the order, the machination. She stopped there, and I came to rest beside her.

"Do you feel like sitting down?" she asked.

I sat down.

"That's better, isn't it?"

I nodded.

The sun shook behind her shoulders—I squinted up at her—she laughed in the wind.

Erich joined us on the hill. He looked at me, then at Miriana. Then they both sat down in the dirt and we formed a triangle. Miriana got to work sifting sand through her fist.

"The factory misses you," said Erich.

"I'm sorry," I said. I began to tear up. "I never meant to let you down," I said. I was very hot on the hill. Sweat, freed from my brow, dripped into my eyes. I was six years old, maybe younger. I couldn't make eye contact with Erich, afraid of his wrath. I looked at Miriana, who returned my gaze. She was biting her bottom lip and kneading the sand with her fingers. The eye contact was comforting.

"You have been a big disappointment to us," said Erich. "A big fucking disappointment."

I started to cry.

"That's enough, Erich," said Miriana.

I cried harder for her compassion.

"Aren't you always going on about the 'erotics of suffering'? Erich said.

Miriana reached over and stroked my cheek. She wiped a tear away. It clung to her fingertip. She blew it into the sand.

"I'd like to explain something to you," she said. She leaned toward me with poor posture, slouching. "You must listen very hard. Are you ready?"

I nodded.

"When you are finished listening, you will be a different man. Are you ready to be a different man?"

I nodded again.

"At the beginning," said Miriana, "there was God. Then there was man. Are you following so far?"

I tried to nod a third time but my skull was frozen to my neck. She wiped a slick of drool from my chin.

"This is a waste of time," said Erich.

"The first man had dimension. Dimensions. Length times width times height. He had color—his descendants called it race. At the beginning, there was one ideal set of dimensions and an ideal color. A man like you found in Greece and Italy. And there was Germania, too. The ideal man is 183 centimeters tall. Proportion is historical truth. When facts are corrupted, it's called entropy. Do you like bedtime stories?"

I missed my mother.

"Good boy. The men from these places were trans-historical. They've always been among us. It's not surprising that the strongest nations on Earth have the highest populations of original men. Some of us came here. But not everyone was following their historical imperative. Like the men from Greece and Italy, like us. Some people came here because Duma was once open to all peoples. It was a sandbox—a place for global outsiders to practice their ideologies, to churn theory into reality. Right here in the desert. A sandbox with infinite resources. Funded by global enterprises. Predicated on the notion that when all needs are satisfied, what emerges is the socialist utopia. Thousands arrived. Idealists, but also opportunists, objectivists.

"There erupted an ugly chaos. A group consolidated power over others; it used violence and the categorical imperative of racial superiority to manipulate and subjugate the weaker groups. This happened organically, through the inevitable sorting that occurs when one group maintains a superior biological profile. We manufactured tragedies and burned scapegoats. Antisemitism and racism weren't part of the design but the inevitable devolution of an experimental paradigm. The utopian structures devolved into structures of control. The tenets of modernism—the rejection of history, the rejection of the real—are seedlings in the Garden of Eden; as they grow, they can be chained, wired, and shaped like bonsai trees, until they become the great oaks of totalitarianism. Do you understand, little one?

"We brought our own knowledge to Duma, our own theory. That pluralism is a myth; it's not how humanity is constructed. Our theory breathes life into the cast concrete of the buildings around you. We used theory to build Duma into a clean, white acropolis, a spiritual and architectural return to order, without caricature and distortion, without the chains of degenerative Enlightenment thinking. It is our Gesamtkunstwerk. Duma is the spectacular failure of the modern world."

Her voice left dust in the air.

"You really are wasting your time," said Erich.

"He'll come around. I know he will."

"They're constitutionally incapable."

"What about me?"

Erich was silent. I felt I could help.

"I'm only sleepy," I said. My eyelids were very heavy. Miriana brought my head to her lap. She stroked my hair. My eyes closed.

"Dearest," she said. "Tell us who is making the pamphlets."

"Margarette Khvalsky," I said. A rush of warmth. A cool breeze. Her breast above.

A sense of despair.

"See? That wasn't so bad."

Erich's face appeared next to Miriana. I saw their minds through the holes in their noses. They argued about what to do with my body and me. Then Miriana kissed Erich on the corner of his mouth and slapped him gently.

"If it's working, then why isn't he in the factory right now?" said Erich. "Then why did he leave?"

"He's obstinate. That's what makes him valuable."

"One has to arrive at it honestly, like you did. You can't fake it. You have to, I don't know, have a predilection for it. A knack. A knack for fascism."

"Don't use that word. I loathe that word."

"It's what it is. It's what we're doing."

"We're making *art*," she said, sneering. She looked off into the distance to gather herself, then turned back to Erich. "*You're* theory," she said. "I'm praxis."

"What does that mean? What the fuck does that even *mean?*"

Miriana lifted my shirt and ran her hand in circles over my stomach; her palm was cool and wet against my skin.

"Little Zelnik?"

"Mm."

"Soon you will go to the Agricultural District. There, you will—"

Erich interrupted her. "What are you doing? Just let him go to the factory. He's not going to need your stupid—"

Miriana slapped him, then turned back to me. She squeezed my face between her bracketed hands.

"In the Agricultural District, you will find a mirror and see your true self. This person will alarm you at first. Do not be afraid. Walk from there and find a staircase. Descend. The staircase will take you into an altered sphere where you will experience your true self. Your true self is strong and violent. Your true self will want to kill, to insist on your power over others. This power is honest and forgivable and nonnegotiable. Nature is sympathetic to this power. You will meet people down there, people from your world. People from your life. From your family. You will end your world by ending them. If you emerge from this place, you will emerge as your true self, stronger than ever. You will be adopted by our family. You will put your power to use. You will do what we ask you to do."

She let go of my face, then stroked my cheek with the back of one of her long fingers.

"Do you understand?"
The breeze was points of light on my skin.
I understood.

I woke up with a terrible, woozy hangover and stayed in bed for an hour with my head beneath the pillow. The headache kept me from forming cogent thoughts; instead, my mind cascaded through images pulled randomly from my subconscious. Uncle with a square of toilet tissue stuck to his shoe; a sandy path at dusk; a snuff box with spilled contents; my mother at the kitchen table, smoking, her curly hair dusty in the afternoon light.

I dressed for work. It took me a while to find the uniform I'd been assigned—it had been crumpled behind the bathroom door, evidently unworn for quite some time. The air outside was cool. It was the first time in recent memory that I didn't start immediately sweating after leaving the Crescent. I walked toward Beau Gino Plaza, enjoying the weather. People around me seemed content. I had a pain in my stomach that I was trying to ignore. I walked a little behind a pair of workers, absorbed by the satisfying crunch of their boots on the pebbled path. The cuffs of their trousers were badly frayed. They were having a sociable argument over a shared recollection. One asserted that his memory was correct; the other objected. They competed over who remembered best the number of the bus that was to take them to the Agricultural District.

"We go there every day!" said one of them. "How can you not remember?"

# A BRUTAL DESIGN

It was a valid, if unanswerable, question.

They continued in this vein until the three of us reached the Plaza. Off they went to the bus terminal. I watched them approach a group of fellows under the brick half-shell and ask around. The argument was settled. One of the workers celebrated by pumping his fist above his head as if he were leading a revolution; the other moped sullenly.

The Agricultural District sounded interesting to me. The phrase scraped across my mind like silverware on a dinner plate. "Agricultural District." I said it out loud and had a strange feeling that I had spent my whole life moving in that direction but had been interrupted, and now I was coming back to it, like returning to a dream after using the bathroom. I felt bad for those men, concerned with trivial matters like bus numbers. How limited must their lives be to argue about such things. For my part, I had purpose: I had a job. A job that I liked. A job I could sink my body into, a tactile experience, instantly gratifying—gratifying dozens of times an hour. The anticipation of the factory made me jumpy. My hands clenched and released; they were beginning to assemble parts that were not yet in their grasp.

I waited impatiently for my bus to arrive, and when it did, I sat in the front row, nearest to the door. I searched my vocabulary for the right word to describe my condition and arrived at "jolly." I let myself go. I seldom let myself go. But today I did. I allowed myself to feel jolly, ejaculating a giggle into the wind. I watched the desert shoot past and took in the kommandant's office dispassionately, like seeing a distant relative at the park and forgoing the effort of connection. I glanced over my shoulder at the other workers on the bus; they sat in rows by themselves; none of them chatted. I felt like making small talk, so I leaned over and nudged the driver. A young man, swimming in his khaki uniform. The starched fabric bunched around his waist like a crumply boil. I wanted to strike the right balance of workplace professionalism and informal comradery.

"Mondays are the worst," I said.

The driver slowly swiveled his face so he could peer at me in his periphery. "It's Thursday."

"Thursday, huh? Thursdays, too," I said.

"What happens on Thursdays?"

"Exactly," I said. "Exactly. Same work, different day."

"That is correct," said the boy driver.

Satisfied, I enjoyed the rest of the drive with a bit of pleasing introspection. Then, abruptly, I was seated on my stool at Row F in Factory 7A, next to Jan and across from—

"Apologies," I said. I tapped on the counter, interrupting the dance of her hands. "Pardon me." She looked up blankly. "I didn't catch your name."

"Daša."

"Ah, Daša," I said, grinning. "I'm going to beat you." I held two parts in front of her and clicked them into place ostentatiously. "The game is afoot," I said. She didn't care.

I worked hard. And fast. So fast that it became necessary to bring the crate from its space near my feet onto the worktable; I was losing too much time bending over, depositing my assemblages. After an hour or so, I noted with much satisfaction how I had begun to lap Daša. For every crate of assemblages she brought to the belt, I brought two. Old man Jan emptied one crate for every four of mine. He sank into his shoulders as he worked, his knotty hands occasionally smushing the cartilage of his weather-beaten nose. After emptying a crate, I had to collect the next sheet of assemblage specifications from the foreman at the northern wall of the floor. The foreman wore the same khaki jumpsuit as we all did, only hers had a pair of green stripes sewn onto each shoulder. The epaulets were lush green. I was obscenely jealous.

"Cushy gig, right?" I said, pulling my next assemblage list from the stack.

"Excuse me?" She was ponytailed so tightly that her follicles appeared to be palpitating.

"How'd you get the job?"

"Same as everyone else," she said. She turned back to her work—what was her work? Guarding the stack of assemblage assignments? She didn't even have a stool to sit on. I looked down at her shoes; a pale red pinky toe jutted out of the broken toecap.

"Want to trade?" I asked.

She sighed deliberately—a sigh forged from molten rock.

"Guess not," I said. "Listen, you may as well give me a second assignment sheet. I'll be done with this one in an hour. It would save me some time. Let me be more efficient, you know? See, what if I finish my current assignment sheet but I've still got room in my crate for a few more assemblages? I'd have to come all the way back over here for my next sheet, a waste of time since I'd have to get up again only a few minutes later once my crate was filled. Do you see what I am getting at?"

She didn't respond, so I decided to help myself to another sheet. When she saw what I was doing, she looked me in the eyes and began to open her mouth, mechanically, as if it was being cranked open like a drawbridge. When it opened to the point where I could see her uvula, vibrating like a rung church bell, she screamed, a ripping, deafening shriek. I drew back violently, hitting my back against a support column. Her mouth remained open for a while after she had stopped screaming—then it closed, her lower jaw cranked back into place. She then returned to her post, that is, staring out at the factory floor and blinking. I looked around. No one seemed to have noticed.

At Row F, I observed how the workers at my table all appeared to me like background characters in a film. Extras. People whose lives, for one brief, fateful moment, intersect with the life of the camera—or the life of the person in the camera's gaze. It was all about focus. I found myself closing one eye and then the other, shifting the focal point, or squinting to contract the depth of field. Daša in parallax.

I did this for a while, then remembered I was supposed to be working. But the problem was that I didn't want to anymore. I'd lost too much momentum. The foreman's scream had left me feeling shaken, somehow both lucid and groggy. It ricocheted around in my head. I dug my finger into my ear and wiggled it, trying to release the scream, but it stayed put.

In the bathroom, I splashed cold water on my face and appraised my reflection. Other than a boil on my neck which pumped with pain when I grazed it, I looked normal. Familiar. The lights above the sink were bright. I walked the halls of Factory 7A: I wanted the blood in my hands and legs to get some good circulation; I thought perhaps poor circulation had caused my loss of steam. I roamed the halls, entering rooms, opening doors—nobody minded. I said hello to the people I saw, and they said hello in response. It was a genial time. I passed the Site Manager's office but didn't want to intrude on Mr. Kamwendo. He was a busy man, I knew. One day, I would have a job like his, and I'd appreciate it very much if people wouldn't barge in at all hours just to say hello.

I thought it was prudent to return to work, so I did. I sat at my stool, fidgeted until I was comfortable—I had an itch at the waistline that I could not satisfy—then futzed with a few assemblages. Jan had fallen asleep on one of his. A trickle of his drool lacquered the metal. I jostled him awake.

"Wake up, Jan!" I said.

"Hm?" He glanced around in a confused panic, his hands shaking out in front of him.

"You fell asleep, old man!"

Jan raised his eyes like he was peering over eyeglasses, then turned to dry his assemblage against his uniform.

I let him have it.

"Don't fall asleep again, Jan! Don't make me look bad!" I dove back into my work. Filled a crate. Dumped the assemblages on the belt. Got a new sheet, careful not to ruffle the foreman's feathers again, and started on the new list. I worked for about ten minutes. Then I got up again.

I was restless. I paced the corridor. I looked under the flaps on the belt to see where the assemblages were going. The tunnel disappeared into the factory wall, the assemblages into darkness. I left the floor to see if I could track it but the closest I could get in that direction was a maintenance room messy with tools and cleaning supplies. I pushed around some of the industrial junk with my shoe and snagged it on a bunch of rags.

But they weren't just rags!

I knelt to free my shoe—and found the missing half of my uncle's jacket. I couldn't believe it had turned up. I guessed that it had been repurposed for cleaning. Served him right: his clothes should be for cleaning, not wearing. What felt like joy at finding the missing half very quickly morphed into rage. My stupid uncle. If I saw him, I'd kill him.

The quitting bell rang. As we waited outside for the buses back to Duma, I thought that I'd probably wound up in a dead heat with Daša given how far ahead I was. So what if I slacked off a little? The numbers at the end of the day were all that mattered. Bottom lines. That was everything.

I stood in line behind two workers with terribly frayed trouser bottoms. They were engaged in a debate

## A BRUTAL DESIGN

regarding which bus was the proper one for a particular destination.

"Bus *fifteen* takes you to the athletic fields," said the taller, balder one. "It's *sixteen* that takes you to the Agricultural District."

"You nitwit," said the shorter, hairier one. "*Sixteen* is for the athletic fields. But now *fifteen* is Agricultural District."

The taller one massaged his forehead. "How can you not remember? We go there every day."

I interrupted them with a laugh. "Fellows," I said, placing my arms around their shoulders and inserting my head between them. I recognized them from my earlier commute. "My dear fellows, you were having the same argument just this morning. Now, if you go to the Agricultural District every day, then what are you doing *here*?"

The men looked at each other and shrugged.

"We go sometimes," said one.

"Yeah, we go sometimes," said the other.

The bus arrived.

# TEN

I N THE MORNING, after a night of dreams about the Agricultural District, I stopped in the center of Beau Gino Plaza on my way to the bus depot and looked up at the library. I had not really looked at the library before. Its eighty-foot façade of reinforced glass loomed over the Plaza, elevated on concrete pylons, accessible by a cement staircase. Its face of glass asked me inside. I politely declined, saying I had work to get to. The voice in my head, speaking for the library, reminded me that I had done a terrific job yesterday and that I could take the morning off. I agreed.

Cold air blew across my face as I entered. Librarians in green-and-red plaid skirts and black turtlenecks bussed carts of books through the aisles. A frightening man in a dark suit eyed me from behind his concrete block desk. I nodded at him and passed by confidently. I wasn't looking for anything in particular. I was happy to smell the lignin and listen to the library's quietude. I walked slowly through the stacks, letting my fingers dance along the spines of the books, letting their titles flow through me as if I were using the raw material of text as fuel for my movement. I couldn't recall the last book I'd read.

The main floor had a soaring ceiling made of (what else) cast concrete waffling, and in the center there was a massive square skylight. There was enough dust kicked up and swirling around the place that the contours of the light were visible, a column descending to the floor. I was enchanted. I loved the interplay between the massive square of writhing sunlight and the relative darkness surrounding it. It was perfect architecture; I wished I could measure up to it and felt sad that I would always be a member of an imperfect type, the type that gets subjugated by Erich's type. I followed the aisle of books until it deposited me back where the dirty white concrete of the atrium was awash in flaming sunlight.

But where I thought I would find solid floor, I found, in fact, a square the same dimensions as the skylight: an empty space, a cutaway, a massive drop. I peered over the lip of the void and down into a square pool of water two stories below. There was no railing or warning; just a void where the floor would have been. Around the pool below a dozen people sat in patio furniture smoking cigars and sipping drinks. They wore suits or military uniforms with ornamental fabrics on their breasts and shoulders.

I thought perhaps I could check out a book on the Agricultural District, so I asked one of the passing librarians what section that would be under. The librarian stopped wheeling her cart and touched the tight bun on the back of her head.

"A bus can get you there," she said. She pointed toward the front door then touched her bun again. "If you walk west several kilometers you can follow signs for the *zemes ukio rajonas. Is ten pamatysite grudu elevatorius. Aš nevaldau. Prašau nužudyti—*"

"I'm sorry, could you slow down?"

"Yes?"

"I think you slipped into a different language," I said.

"Oh?" She evened a row of books with one hand. Her suggestion seemed to be that I go to the Agricultural District and conduct my *own* research.

"Which bus is it?" I asked.

"To go to Agricultural District? In the grain elevators."

A pattern began to light up in my mind. Not everyone here was doing okay.

"How does one get there?"

"There is a bus that can take you."

"Which bus is it?" I asked. "Fifteen or sixteen?" The librarian looked down through the empty space at the pool below.

"I wish to swim," she said.

"What would happen if you jumped?"

The librarian tilted her head back and laughed. Her neck was ringed with creases. I could see the red roof of her mouth, the curving white marble of her teeth. She seemed to have really enjoyed my comment. A tear hovered, stuck, in the corner of her right eye. She began to wheel the cart away, but I held her elbow. She turned to me with a blazing face.

"What bus is it?" I said. I was afraid of the feeling of her bones through the thin wool turtleneck sleeve.

She pushed her face close to mine and said, "I would drown." When she smiled, blood swirled through her cheeks. I released her. She wheeled her cart of books away.

I left the library and loitered around the bus terminal asking folks for the bus number. Someone knew, eventually. I sat down in the dust to wait, leaning against the arched wall of glazed brick rather than sitting on the uncomfortable boulder that was supposed to be a bench. I was confused by the depth of my sorrow but then I realized it was coming from the part of me that was late for work at Factory 7A. I had a novel thought that I could live with sorrow. Others came and waited near me, chatting in their bad English, laughing. One person, a lanky man in a gray utility suit, was particularly happy. He procured a case of cigarettes from his pocket and offered them around. Everyone, including me, took one. We all shook his hand, slapped his shoulder, patted him on the back. It seemed like he had just received a promotion or his wife had just given birth to a healthy girl. I was happy to enjoy a cigarette and to be included in his joy. I couldn't remember the last time I'd smoked one. But as I inhaled, I felt a terrible itch at the waistline of my trousers, on the right side of my body, above my hip bone. I scratched and scratched until finally, rising, I excused myself and walked around the half-shell of the bus terminal for privacy. I pulled my pants down to get a better look and found a neat line of raised red bites with clear incision points in their centers. There were three of them total, in a diagonal line, spaced like the stars in Orion's belt. I dug my thumbnail into each of them in two directions, depressing an X into the center of the bite. I had learned the trick somewhere; I couldn't remember where. Somewhere I had lived among bugs. The X at the heart of each bite alleviated the painful itching somewhat. The smoke from the cigarette wafted into my eyes. I pulled my trousers back up and rejoined the men on the other side of the terminal. The sun was high in the sky and the men were crowded under the brick half-shell now, enjoying the shade. There was no room for me and they didn't look eager to accommodate. Their joy had left them. I paced alongside the terminal. The waist of my pants chafed against the bites with each step. It wasn't much longer until the bus sputtered to a stop in front of us and we climbed on. I found a spot a few rows from the back and dislodged the window from the grime that wedged it in place.

We rumbled out of the plaza to the west. I sat back and tried to enjoy the ride, but once we'd picked up enough speed, the breeze began slinging pebbles and sand in through the window. I sidled farther toward the aisle where I could still feel some of the air. The bites on my waist were insufferable. I rubbed my waistline so the fabric bristled against the bites. It only made it worse. I closed my eyes, trying to lose myself in the droning rumble. Eventually the histaminic activity subsided, but it wasn't long until the relief from itching gave way to an awareness of hunger. I tried to think of the last meal I'd had, the last food I'd ingested. I couldn't come up with it. I was suddenly starving.

The bus disgorged us at the edge of a field. The soil was dry and cracked and a few puny stalks of stiff yellow wheat shook in the breeze. A colossal industrial building of gray concrete lorded it over the fields, with smaller agronomical structures dotting the grounds beneath like its juvenile offspring. Sections of its wall were collapsed, exposing its steelwork bones. Rusted staircases snaked up and down its sides. A covered chute the color of rusted copper spanned the air between two silos. It looked like a dilapidated, mutated grain elevator.

I fell in behind the men from the bus as they cut through a field. They let their hands bounce from stalk to stalk, occasionally snapping one at the waist, crumbling the dry spindle to powder beneath their boots. Their demeanor had changed. No chatting now, no cigarettes smoked. They walked almost in formation through the baked field until they came to a paved road that led beneath the shadow of the looming structure. I glanced through the holes in the structure into the darkness.

Soon we approached one of the smaller outposts, which I now saw to be a covered shack with a counter and service window. A foreign word was scrawled into the thatch above the window and a woman was seated behind the counter. She watched us approach with a drained expression, like lifeless marble statuary. Her red hair was ironed straight, encasing her face in parentheses. She preempted us with a shrug.

"Nothing today."

"What do you mean nothing?" said the man who had provided the cigarettes. His English was worse with anger.

The purveyor shrugged again. "It's like I said."

"Then what's that?"

"This?" She pointed to the heel of black bread on the counter next to her. "This is for me." She exposed an incomplete row of teeth.

The cigarette man threw his hands up and cursed in his native tongue. He turned and consulted with his peers. They evidently didn't understand what had transpired and were just as upset when he translated the news. I was impressed by his brazen flaunting of the linguistic rules. I watched them argue from a distant vantage, disconnected from their difficulty. I didn't need what they needed. I decided, too, that I didn't need to eat, even though I was famished. I watched the circle they had formed: it shifted in emotional spasms that spread from one man to the other and then back again. Their bodies formed an order of sticks that swayed with feeling. It occurred to me that their clothes hung off their bodies, making them appear like flickering sails. They swam in the collars of their utility suits; their collarbones ran in vast ridges across their concave chests. I saw the skulls behind their faces.

They deliberated for another moment—the cigarette man tossed a foreign expletive at the woman, which caused one of his peers to grab his arm and reprimand him—and then they walked off en masse. I followed. They didn't seem to mind that I was tagging along. They were adroit at minding their own business. I observed how the last of their group dragged his right foot across the dirt; it jutted out to the side.

We followed the path around the structure and startled a flock of grackles nesting in the exposed metalwork. They flew off into the bowels of the building in a shrieking flutter. My stomach cramped urgently, and I wondered if there might be a toilet somewhere inside. I stopped on the sandy path, letting the group of men heading away from the structure, into another field rife with desiccated wheat. I wondered about the kind of work they were to perform and how long they had been performing it. Their bronze heads bobbed above the wheat, disintegrating.

I climbed over the broken concrete and entered the building, keeping my focus on the splotches of light that appeared through the crumbling walls, waiting for my eyes to adjust. It was cool inside, and water dripped from invisible pipes. I put my feet in shallow puddles and walked from chamber to chamber in search of the facilities. Each room was filled with decrepit agricultural machinery. Grains of wheat stuck to the soles of my sodden shoes. I came into a room big enough to house a broken-down combine. Most of its pale blue paint had worn away. There was loose grain strewn about the cab and its blades were rounded and useless. To get to the next room I had to hug the brick wall to avoid stepping in the fetid black liquid that had oozed out of a burst barrel. I looked down as I passed and saw my reflection in the rancid slop.

I came to a cavernous hallway that connected to other sectors. By now I felt feverish. I held my body tightly as I ran down the hallway, pushing open each door I passed along the way. Finally, one yielded the dank tiling of a restroom. I entered the closest stall and pulled down my trousers and released. Foul toilet water splashed out of the bowl and onto my legs, but I didn't care. My head lolled backwards, my abdominal muscles contracting painfully. I stared at the ceiling, tracing the network of piping, following its vectors along the wall and down to the basin at the back of the toilet. I fought the urge to lose consciousness and then I fought the urge to see what I had passed. There was no tissue and the flushing mechanism did nothing.

What was wrong with me?

The awful water settled between my legs. I breathed until I felt strong enough to stand, which I did by placing my hands flat against the walls of the stall and pushing outward. When I knelt to pull up my trousers, I found more bites on my waist; I counted five new ones. I realized they were louse bites. They itched so badly I wanted to cut them out of my skin.

I stumbled out of the stall and grasped the sink counter but couldn't see my face through the lamina of dust on the mirror. I drew my palm across it, revealing someone I at once recognized as the person that was really me. But I couldn't remember ever seeing this person before—this version of me. I scanned my shocked face. My eyes were small and black and quivered with terror; my cheekbones tented a thin sheet of flesh. Dirty sweat gathered in the tide pools of my skeletal clavicle. Across my face: little burst novae of subcutaneous blood, a galaxy of blemishes, patches of wiry hair, signs of disease, nutritional deficiencies, indigo, purple, scarlet, black.

I could remember nothing in
time I blinked I
felt myself wa
ke up blinked and hop
ing I would awak
e in bed; at home; wi
th Uncle; with Moth
er and Father;
but I was here;

it was now and now I looked like this is what I looked like.

I stepped away and began to cry. Crying, I fled the bathroom and tried to find my way out of the structure, making a series of impulsive turns that took me deeper into the building. Tears blurred my vision. The rust and brick and concrete and steel fused into an industrial palette I couldn't see through. I plowed through rooms littered with garbage, materials, equipment, hardware. I tripped and fell into pools of stagnant water and oil and worse. I careened into walls and door jambs; I cut myself repeatedly on exposed nails. I couldn't stop crying. I came to a shaky metal staircase that led below. I grabbed the rusted handrail and flung myself down it, taking the steps two at a time until one of them broke off and I tumbled through it and crashed through eroded wooden floorboards and landed on a pile of wet thatch.

Dust stormed around me from the fall and I rested.

For several minutes I couldn't feel any pain. I breathed deeply, calmly. I was no longer crying. In fact, I felt like laughing. I could only imagine what I had looked like, flailing around the factory like I was Buster Keaton until collapsing through the floor and knocking myself out.

Water dripped onto my face. I heard a faint electrical buzzing sound on the outskirts of my hearing. It was familiar to me. I thought back to something I had learned at Sizenko, in one of my science classes—would it have been biology? or maybe physics?—that memory is best triggered through smell, but hearing is second-best. A song from the radio, a random piece of a melody, was enough to send me back to where I was when I first heard it, how I was feeling when I first heard it. How was I feeling when I'd first heard this faint electrical buzzing? Where was I? I closed my eyes and concentrated on the noise, hoping to find a ledge in my mind to hoist myself up with, to see from a great height the topography of memories, the islands and rivers and hammocks of trees—Uncle was there, and Erich was there, and Professor Hallen and Zofia were there, and...there was nothing beyond them. I squinted to see further, and there were the campuses of Sizenko and Barnova. I couldn't see further than that, and I couldn't see any details, any nuances, any clarities. Where were the rest of these memories?

With trouble, I rose from the pile of thatch, pausing with my hand against the cold brick wall for support while my body reapportioned its blood. I began to follow the buzzing, stopping every dozen or so steps to make sure it was still gaining in volume. I pushed through door after door, room after room, climbing over and around broken pallets and farming equipment, until I came to a high-ceilinged room in the center of which stood, at a slashing angle, a train carriage.

The polished wooden slats of the car had been painted a blazing red and lacquered; even in the slim twitching light of a hanging lamp they shone. The metal handrails on either side of the sliding door were polished, too, and felt cool and clean beneath my hands. I pulled myself onto the foothold of the wagon and tried the door, which flung open after significant effort. The space inside was quite small, a modest rectangle, made for five or six cows at most. Dust particles swirled in the wind from the opening door.

It was a pristine specimen, too flawless for its surroundings, certainly not a train car that had seen any recent action. I orbited the carriage several times, observing it from different angles, trying to get a sense of its objectivity. Then I scanned the walls of the room, running my palm along the dirty concrete, looking for seams that would suggest how such a large object could have come to rest here. I found no seams. But then it hit me: the piece had been created on site. Either it had been disassembled, transported, and reassembled; or it had been fabricated here altogether. The latter theory excited me so much that I hopped up and down on my toes. It wasn't an echt train car; it was a work of art! I hopped back over to the hand-rails, pulled myself back up, and knocked on the door: it

## ZACHARY C. SOLOMON

was synthetic wood! I was awed, overcome, emotional. I lingered close to the synthetic wood, then jumped down to find what I was sure was there: the eggshell-white museum plaque.

### Reproduction of Căile Ferate Române Cattle Wagon

Miriana Grannoff

Artificial wood, iron, rubber, metal, acrylic, lacquer, plexiglass

I read the plaque several times. Glanced at the wagon, read it again. I wondered what process rendered a work of art a memorial, as distinct from an homage. Was it where you stood? Was it context alone? There were places on Earth where terrible tragedies had occurred. Minds had conspired to preserve those places in situ, altering nothing. Letting the site of tragedy remain the same could serve as signifier, reminder, and warning all at once; it could inspire the prevention of similar tragedies. It is one thing to stand on the floor of a museum and read about the tragedy; it is another entirely to stand in the tragedy itself, receiving its ambient vestiges as they seep through the wet grass into your socks.

How weak the threshold between memorial and homage. Why couldn't a person—not me, but another—visit the site of tragedy and feel *inspired* by it? Enlightened? Think to himself: this was the site of a success. This was the site of an accomplishment.

I thought about the rest of Miriana's art that I'd seen around Duma. The lamps and the military office in the desert. Visiting those images, I heard words echo in my mind—words in Miriana's voice.

*modern*

*praxis*

*raw*

The voice disturbed me.

I left the room with the train car and followed the ever-present buzzing deeper into the structure's basement, wondering at myself, at my actions, my sense of agency in the world. For the first time in my life I felt that my movements were predetermined, felt that I had no choice in the matter, felt myself surrendering to the currents. Felt myself watching myself move deeper into the structure, following the ever-present buzzing. Felt the cable connecting my sternum to the void. Wherever it was taking me, that place would not yield what it was that I wanted.

I stopped, at last, at yet another staircase that corkscrewed down into the darkness below the floor. A modernist, concrete staircase—that *style*—brutalist, the defeat of nature at the hands of modern man. I used to love things like this. I used to love how order was superimposed over the jungle. I much preferred the jungle now.

I wasn't surprised to find yet another off-white museum plaque attached to the wall just beyond the staircase.

**Life Is Cheap**
Miriana Grannoff
Concrete, wood, carpet, felt, mineral fiber, halogen,

plastic, glass, oxygen, plexiglass, saliva, blood, hair, cardboard, metal, etc.

I descended to the first step; the buzzing ceased. There was only darkness below. I took the stairs one at a time.

The carpet, forever, damp, yellow, forever, beneath my feet.

As I walked, I thought a lot about Zofia Percik, whom Uncle did not approve of, though she wasn't exactly the sort of person who required one's approval and would have scoffed at it had it been presented to her.

It hardly mattered.

There was so much time down there. I spent all of it thinking and walking. Every time I turned a corner I faced more of the same. Every door I opened led to the rear of the same room. Was it what life was really like? An ouroboric illusion of movement?

I grew tired of my stupid thoughts.

I grew tired of the fantasy arguments I had with you in my head. It was *your* voice I heard. Not my mother's, not my father's. Yours.

I used to write letters to you. I must have written hundreds of letters to you over the years. It was the only way I could get those terrible arguments out of my head. The only way to tell you the truth. To expose myself. Make myself vulnerable. Whenever I finished a letter to you, I would drop it wherever I was: beneath an oak tree in Drndić Park, through the trash chute in the cafeteria, between the pages of a textbook in the library of the Architectural Institute. They weren't for you to read, though I guess a part of me wanted you to read them—the self-saboteur inside me. I always addressed and stamped the letters, but I never put a return address on them. So unless a nosy Samaritan found one and mailed it, you never saw them. It was helpful to me to address them to you but not send them. It felt as useful as sending.

But sometimes, like now, I had to write letters to you in my mind. I visualized the stationary, the bloodlike streak of my black-ink fountain pen where I lingered too long on the page so the blot stained through the cardstock, visualized your name and address, visualized licking the envelope's adhesive strip. I wondered if any of my letters had ever made it to you. You would never have admitted to it if one had.

In all honesty, I wrote to you because I loved you and I cared about you. I thought sometimes about how you kept the radio on all night, to have a reassuring presence in your drafty room off the kitchenette. The wind always seemed to blow from the east, through the alley next to Mela and Elam's house, across Alizabet Street, and directly into your bedroom. I used to think you kept the radio on so loudly to keep me from sleeping, too, to keep one of us awake just in case we needed to leave in the night. But after our argument about it, which I won, you began to sleep with the radio switched off, and your night terrors returned. You would wake up screaming horrid, despairing, dream-filled screams, your voice bellowing and choking and rasping like you were swallowing water. A scream direct from your subconscious. Nothing was more horrific than the sound of your voice when you screamed, the sound of an ancient, biblical terror. A terror you couldn't fake, say, for the sake of revenge. I preferred your full-decibel Haydn and Mozart concertos over that any night.

There was another thing I would have told you if you were down there with me, and that was about the design—the one that got me here in the first place.

You see, I drew plans for a new temple to replace the one in which my parents were trapped and burned to death—your brother and sister-in-law. I imagined it at the exact same location on the small side street on the periphery of Saint Marya Square. The main building of the temple would resemble its predecessor, with a wattle and daub exterior, whitewashed, a humble agrarian look, a humble mahogany barn door, dormer windows with grass-green shutters. A nondescript, almost invisible one-story building consisting of two main rooms: a prayer hall and a gathering hall. Inside the prayer hall were a pair of humble wooden beams that supported the ceiling, and a makeshift bimah that would be one step high and wide enough for a pair of feet held close together.

But surrounding it was a six-foot-tall wall made of thick shatter-proof glass—not so much a wall as a container in the shape of a wall, running the perimeter of the temple. And inside of the glass container wall would be a bed of ever-smoldering embers, blackened rocks, and low-burning wood fires. The fires would be fed by a subterranean gas line. The fire would burn all year long, never resting, serving as the temple's exterior *ner tamid*, the eternal flame, as the building would have no electricity and could not support an electric bulb inside. The wall of embers would act as a barrier against further fire.

I drew the design for this temple in the workshop of the Architectural Institute. You didn't know this story—how could you? I carried the design out of the campus in my briefcase. It was after ten at night. I was stopped by a patrol of gendarmes for violation of curfew.

It astonished me what walking through that maze was dredging up. Something about being down there emancipated my memory.

The gendarmes—one of them had a cigarette dangling from his lips, the other one wore goggle-like sunglasses that ensconced his eyes from all sides—had escorted me to an office inside of the Speer-inspired police headquarters. I was brought into an interrogation room and given an uncomfortable chair behind a long wooden table. They took my briefcase and emptied its contents on the table. When they saw the temple design, they took that, along with the other papers I had, and left me alone in the room. A few pens and scraps of worthless paper were all that was left. I sat for several hours in the gloom, thinking it was the end for me. I took up the pen and smoothed out one of the papers, intending to make a will of some kind, but nothing came to me. I had no valuable possessions, and whatever I did own would fall to you automatically. There was no other family.

Eventually the guards returned, along with a third person, a bureaucrat in a suit who took the chair opposite me. He placed my temple design on the table and turned it so it was oriented to me. He put his finger on it and asked me if I knew that designs like this were contraband. Of course I knew, I told him. I knew what happened when you entered the police headquarters. I didn't have anything to gain from lying.

I wonder if you have heard about a place called Duma? he asked. I had. Your letter had arrived only a couple of weeks before that, a brick of incoherent rambling, fanatical and euphoric, the voice of a man under the sway of a movement. What it lacked in cogent detail it made up for in sweaty, smudgy fervor. I had to admit to myself that the letter had done more than intrigue me. I couldn't imagine I would have wound up here without the magnetism of your letter. I hardly recognized your voice in those words—upon reading and rereading the letter, I even thought that maybe you hadn't written it, that it was a ploy to get me to Duma. That idea doesn't seem so far-fetched now.

The man explained Duma to me. The state was giving select persons the opportunity to leave—persons whose "traits," for one reason or another, were incompatible with the State's "traits." There had been a financial incentive for the State to ship some of us off to Duma rather than let us starve to death in a work camp or worse. Duma was an "experiment in the desert," he said, where alternate ideologies could be put into practice without threat, the results of which would be recorded and studied. And if the experiment was successful, those ideologies seen to be the most effective would be piecemeal or wholly implemented in the nations that were cosponsoring the trial.

We think it would be perfect for a free thinker, he said. This place isn't well-suited for people like you.

The bureaucrat asked the gendarmes then to leave us in privacy, which they did. He then loosened his tie and leaned over the table to level with me.

"Now that I can be frank," he said, "I would go too if I could. Duma is freedom. Even our so-called party loyalists want to get out there. Before I came in here, I phoned my contact over there." He tapped my design. "They need an architect. The old one died. Couldn't handle the desert heat." He laughed. "They need an architect who is trained in progressive architecture. This," he said, "is your credential."

He must have sensed hesitation.

"You can come back when your work is finished," he said. "Besides, you've got family there."

I asked how he knew you were there and he tapped his nose.

"I am the State," he said with an ironic bluster.

They prepared a bag for me, and as they drove me to the station, we passed the darkened shoe factory where you'd worked after the lab was forced to let you go. The gendarmes waited with me on the platform until the train arrived. As it pulled into the station, one of them told me not to complain because not everyone gets so lucky. The other one slapped me affectionately on the cheek, but I could see how angry he was, all of that anger shivering in his eyes. He thanked me for my service to our country and saw to it that I was safely on board, the doors closing, before they turned and left through the gate. The woman on the train beside me practiced her English the entire journey. *Long-distance telephone. Long-distance telephone. Long-distance telephone.*

There was nowhere to sit down and rest, but since it was impossible to distinguish one room from the next and the damp carpet kept my feet from hurting, there was no compelling reason to stop walking. Other than exhaustion. But I wasn't there yet.

The buzzing had come back—just a little. Just above nothing, so that I heard it constantly but could never fully concentrate on it, like a bright afterimage burned onto the eye that you chase and chase while it remains always just out of sight.

The yellow carpet was consistent. The walls were clad in awful yellow wallpaper with a motif of stripes and dots. Some rooms had huge, unmovable rolls of musty feltlike carpeting piled against the walls—those rooms were a relief to my eyes. Something new to look at it. When I came across the rolls for the second time, I stopped to examine them more carefully. They were rough against my palms, smelled like smoke. I put my face close to one of the rolls and squinted at the small, wiry hairs. I rubbed my hand against one until I felt static electricity. The hairs marionetted, attached by invisible strings to my palm.

I recognized these as the rolls of felt or carpet that lined the walls of the room in the photograph. The photograph I'd found under my credenza.

The one thing that changed from room to room was the ceiling. In some rooms there was a drop ceiling with monotonous mineral fiber tiling, broken up with banks of harsh fluorescent lighting. Other rooms, however, had ceilings that consisted of a glass mirror, semi-transparent, so that I could see ghostly images beyond the glass through the too-sharp image of my environment. In those rooms, I looked up to see myself lost in carpeting. Carpeting damp enough that if I slept and woke up, my shirt was wet. And it stayed wet as I resumed my walk, clinging to me like a mucus membrane. At least the coolness kept my louse bites from hurting.

At one point I rubbed my hands along my body and felt my ribs emerging through my skin. My body was becoming translucent. My veins were raised, the color of plums. I was cold and hungry. I thought sometimes that the buzzing from the fluorescents was patterned. I detected rhythms, became sure there were little silences, little spaces of dead air that made a syncopation out of the buzzing. If I knew Morse code, I could have interpreted the pattern, but I didn't know Morse code.

After two long rests, waking each time to a deep, gnawing hunger, I came across a room with four people praying and one person dead on the ground. The praying people faced the same direction, billowing like torn flags. They were emaciated, their clothes tattered, their faces gaunt, appalling. They noticed me and grabbed each other, called out to me in desperation, asked me to rescue them—or join them, I couldn't tell. I recognized them immediately—not personally, but I knew that they were from our region, praying with the same accent, speaking in the same dialect, and with a frightful shock it occurred to me that if I were to stay with them, join them in their desperate prayer, then I would be no better than them, they who were asking God for forgiveness and waiting for death.

I fled the room in terror, leaving their voices to be quickly swallowed by the buzzing.

*Your* voice was a constant presence in my mind. I imagined you judging my decisions, my steps—running away from our lantzmen was a big hit with you. You chastised me for a full day after that. How could I abandon our people? Where was my sense of loyalty? Of duty? You prodded me to turn back. And why not? Why didn't I turn around, go back in the direction I came from, find the staircase, and climb out?

Well, I tried. But after I fell asleep for the first time, I lost track of which way was "forward" and which was "backward." There were no patterns. No signifiers. I got confused, paranoid, disoriented. I second-guessed myself repeatedly.

After several more long rests I woke to find a heel of soggy black bread beside me. I picked even its crumbs from the carpet and inhaled them, fibers and all.

# ELEVEN

ZOFIA ENTERED MY THOUGHTS AGAIN. Did you know that Zofia survived the attack in the basement? The bullet passed through her body, just above her hip, missing the bone, tearing only cartilage, flesh, the body's insulation. I tried to visit her in her home, but her father wouldn't let me see her. He said it was my fault she'd been hurt. He had forbidden her from ever seeing me again. He'd known about me, he said. He jabbed me in the sternum with his hairy finger. The Perciks were a proud and loyal family, he told me. Then he slammed the gate in my face. It was snowing, maybe even the first snow of the season. Heavy wet flakes that accumulated on the windshields of cars and rooftops. I pulled down my ushanka, buried my hands in the pockets of my coat, and walked home. It was a little past nine in the morning and the breathing body of an emaciated dog was sprawled in middle of our street. You were making tea in the kitchen when I came in. My face was wet but I can't remember if I had been crying or if it was the snow. My cheeks were red and puffy. My coat wasn't warm enough. You laughed at me and said I was the very picture of the immigrant. Both of your big toes poked out of your socks.

The truth is, I am partially to blame for why you never treated me like family but instead like an immigrant. I had the gall to be the son of dead parents, people you disagreed with on an atomic level. You hated their assertive politics, their hunger to make the country accommodate them and not the other way around. You thought they made themselves too visible. They never understood that their actions reflected not just on themselves but on their entire race. You were embarrassed by their shamelessness. You thought their meetings were a waste of time—selfish, frivolous, and worse—dangerous. You were right, I suppose. I was too young to go to their meetings, to disseminate the literature. I was at Sizenko the day they were forced into the temple. I wasn't home to hear the knock on the door, the door's destruction, followed by the rounding up and the marching and the trapping. And they weren't even believers. None of us were. They didn't raise me with faith. Everyone was rounded up and taken to that temple. Believers and nonbelievers alike. It was pure happenstance that I walked through Saint Marya Square on my way home and saw the smoke. I followed the smoke to the temple and saw you in a crowd of people watching from across the way. You took my hand. You didn't tell me my parents were in there until later. I think about me watching them burn inside and not knowing they were in there, I heard screams, but I didn't recognize them as the screams of my mother and father.

The narrative was being rewritten as I walked. I thought of Ludmila Street, where you had been taken. I hadn't seen you taken personally; it was Mela and Elam who reported the story. I had them repeat the chain of events to me ad nauseum, until finally Elam—or was it Mela?—said, "Enough, what good do the details do you? You'll relive them for the rest of your life anyway." I don't know if he or she was right about that since it's not the rest of my life yet, though I am well on my way.

It turned out that Mela and Elam had spoken to Ludwig, whom they saw at the market, and who had seen you escorted off Ludmila Street by three gendarmes in greatcoats and pith helmets, the whole superior officer affair—and Ludwig had said that they beat you pretty badly right then and there, in full view of the daily shoppers, and that your bag of produce spilled out into the courtyard, and that it took only a split second for starving children to scamper to the ground, ducking between the stalls to steal our carrots and potatoes and mushrooms.

By the time I found the station where they were keeping you, you had already turned into one big bruise. Your lips and eyes were swollen up like the pink poster putty my parents used to tack up flyers at night, and you looked wretched, at the bottom of what resembled human. They gave me one look at you, smacked you around in front of me for good measure, and hauled you off for questioning—about what, I didn't learn until later.

Mela and Elam came by to cook for me—I was about to graduate high school then and had piles of coursework—and we talked about our options for getting you out of prison, but they were mostly airless conversations, delusional. We couldn't cobble together a sufficient amount of bribe money, and everyone agreed that the money would be better suited for my education at Barnova anyway.

Did you know that I went to the prison every other day to see if they would give me news of you? Usually they just ignored me, though sometimes one of the low-level gendarmes, excited by his slice of power, would say, "Who, Zelnik? He's crawling around here somewhere," and then smile with a dripping mouth.

For two years I went daily to get news of you. And then, one day, you came home. Just like that. You showed up at our house on Alizabet Street like you were simply returning from work. Of course, you looked completely different. You were a third the size—you were swimming in the clothes you had been wearing when you were taken—and your face was hollow and your eyes were dull and there were scars all over your face, too. You didn't speak for a full week. You drank a lot of tea and sat at the kitchen table, occasionally listening to the radio. And when you did start to speak, you wouldn't speak to me, only to Mela and Elam. You would disappear into their house for hours and hours and when you returned you still wouldn't say anything to me. I was convinced that you hated me. I would catch you looking at me sometimes with a terrible expression on your face, the kind of expression one reserves for people with whom one has a deep and moralistic disagreement—*How could you believe such drivel?* A disdainful expression.

You kept this up for the next few years. I went to class, went out with friends, sat in my bedroom or in the kitchen doing work, drawing plans; you listened to the radio and stared out the window. We got by on scraps and what I made tutoring. And then you were gone again. Gone here, to Duma, I'd later learn.

But, Uncle Vaska, here is what I want to say to you: I know why they took you. I know what you did. Mela and Elam told me, finally. They said that one day not long after you were released, you came to them, sat in their kitchen, and spoke to them for an hour straight, your tea chilling on its saucer, and when you finished you had them swear that they would never tell me. Of course, Mela and Elam, you know them, they can't keep their mouths shut. Really, it's miraculous they didn't say a peep to me for so long.

They sat me down and said, "Little Samsa, your Uncle Vaska saved your life. It was you they were looking for. You they wanted. He went in your place." You had somehow arranged to serve the time that I should have served for the crimes committed by my parents. You knew that was the new edict—the children of degenerates were held accountable, genetically accountable, for such crimes, as if the parents had bequeathed them the guilt in their will. If, God forbid, I'd already had a child of my own, that child would have been imprisoned too, or more likely killed on the spot since there is no sense in imprisoning a baby. But you arranged to go in my stead. Why they accepted your terms, I don't know. I suppose it's evidence that the whole imperative is based on pseudoscientific racist hokum anyway. Just a bunch of lousy excuses to do what they want.

So: you went instead of me. And you came back half of who you used to be, which wasn't much of a person to begin with, since you were never the favorite and you always seemed to struggle with self-invented obstacles, like a willing Sisyphus who doesn't have time to carve meaning out of his absurd task since he's too busy pointing at himself and saying, "See how hard my life is?"

I got too used to defending myself in imagined arguments in my head whenever I would catch you staring resentfully at me. The resentment? That I hadn't thanked you sufficiently for what you did? How could I? I didn't know what you had done for years. Did you wish you had never made the arrangement in the first place? Did you wish that I had been arrested instead?

What was the point of it? Of taking my place? Your good deed punished you in the end. You could never replace me in the seat of punishment; you were brought here, to Duma, to punish me further, to die at my hands, to *turn me into a monster*. If I had seen you down here, in Miriana's labyrinth, would I have killed you?

Of course not.

Dear Uncle Vaska, I wish that you had never gone to prison in my place. I wish you had consulted me before serving the sentence I received for what my parents did. Because maybe things would have worked out differently. Maybe if I had gone and not you, we would both be in our home right now on Alizabet Street, just back from tea at Mela and Elam's house, or perhaps in from a stroll around Bragusa Park, by the canopy of the floral boulevard.

I thought that I was finally going to die. A welcome development. I came across another man, a man in much worse shape than me. He didn't have the benefit of a shirt or any kind of covering, and his pants were in tatters. Part of his brown, depilated scrotum hung through a tear in the fabric. He had a hooked nose like a fascist monument, explicit and proud rising out of the barrenness of his face.

I found myself jealous of his hat, his one possession, and was ashamed to say that killing him for it flashed through my mind. Uncle had owned a hat just like it, a gray wool flat cap with burgundy checkers. He was huddled in the corner of a room, quivering slightly. When he saw me, he buried his head between his arms and knees and shook violently. He looked like a wild animal and I guessed he thought I did too. I tried to crouch beside him, but my knee popped painfully and I fell on my side. When I finally coaxed the man to look at me, his eyes widened. He told me he recognized me. His eyes flitted across my face; he was searching for the cubbyhole where he kept his memory of what he thought was my face.

"I know your uncle," he said. "Yes, I'm sure of it."

He described your face: blue eyes surrounded by crow's feet; angry, red mouth; a bulbous nose littered with burst capillaries, not unlike the man's own. White tufts of hair above the ears and around the nape, but splotchy bald skin on the top of your head. That's him, I thought.

"Maybe we became one," he said. "The very same."

At that point, I suspected that at least one of us had lost his mind. I reached out to touch him, to see if he was real, but he lashed out and then shriveled away.

I lay on my side and watched him.

"Keep going," he said. "There's an exit."

I wondered why he didn't go himself.

"It's better down here," he said. "For me. For who I am."

I left him in the corner.

The maze changed. The corners disappeared. There was a different kind of light. I came into an atrium with higher ceilings, no mirrors reflecting the maze from above, and I could see the rising bowels of a structure, the interlocking piping, the mess of wiring for the fluorescents. And I saw that some of the interlocking pipes were green and some were silver. And I saw that they were built from the assemblages that were produced in Factory 7A and all the other factories along the avenues in the factory settlement.

Our assembling was for the purposes of art. I remembered that I was *inside* a work of art, remembered the eggshell-white plaque outside the stairs, remembered who had made the art I was dying inside of, her command on the hill. She would see me kill a part of me, my family, where I come from, kill it and find my "true self." Her words were faint but getting stronger, clearer; I saw them, I saw them.

The man I'd left to die.

My stomach had mostly eaten itself and my vision grown mostly dark when I spotted the variation in the repetition. Either I had reached the exit of the maze or the center of it, the farthest possible place from where I began.

If I get out of here, I thought, I will find the ocean. I will go to the pier and see Richard Winger. Maybe he can get me passage on a ship and I can find you, if you're not somewhere in Duma, as everyone says you are. I am beginning to believe that you were never here in the first place.

At last there was a staircase, corkscrewing upward.

The bus rattled to a stop on the far side of the wheat field and I climbed on board. I sat in the first row behind the driver and dislodged the window from its gunky hold, letting the dirty air blow across my face. I could feel the wind contour my cheekbones. There was no one else on board with me. The first stars of the evening were out. If I craned my head, I could see them clearly. I counted a couple of planets and what might have been a satellite. A small, pale dot that moved steadily across the arc of the sky.

I got off in the deserted plaza. A cool wind blew dust across the concrete ground. The shops and stalls were closed. I walked back to the Crescent and let myself in, moving quietly through the curved corridor. It was very hard to walk. There was still a nasty bruise on my hip from where I had fallen. I stopped beneath one of the domed skylights and looked for a while longer at the planets and stars. The sky was distorted in the glass, but I saw a few more of the small pale dots that might have been satellites, blinking as they looped by.

My apartment was in bad shape. The furniture was cracked and holes had appeared in some of it, leaving me with Swiss cheese, or Gaudi architecture. The Formica counter in the kitchenette had begun to detach from its base. I couldn't help but pull the whole thing off to look at the underbelly of sticky, unfinished wood. The slime had reappeared on the windows. Somehow my minifridge had been partially replenished. There were no fruits or vegetables but there were stacks of vacuum-sealed packages containing synthetic meat. I took a few of the packages out, tore apart the plastic, and left them on the counter to warm while I washed my face with the eggy sink water. The fake meat had oxidized by the time I returned to it. Its rouge coloring had turned a scabby brown. I peeled free a slice and sniffed it. It didn't smell bad. I ripped the slice in two and placed half on my tongue. It sizzled like a powdery sugar treat, then melted across my tongue into a pool of iron-flavored saliva. I swished it around, then swallowed. I went back for another slice, then another, then another, until I had finished the whole block and was stuffed. I knew there was a good chance I had been drugged by this meat, but I was too starved to care. I felt bloated and nauseated. I went to the living area to sit, but the cushioned block broke when I sat on it and I fell to the ground, cutting myself on a jagged shard of particle board. I picked some hair out of my teeth and lay on the floor for a few minutes while my heart rate settled down. While I rested, I had the awful sensation that I was forgetting something important.

I was unbearably tired, but the thought of going to sleep was an impossible one, a dream. To think I could lie on my bed and drift away. From nowhere, I remembered telling Miriana and Erich that Margarette had been making the pamphlets. I hoped that Margarette hadn't believed me when I told her I wouldn't rat on her to Erich. She'd had no reason to put her trust in me. It had seemed like the right thing to do was to set her mind at ease, to let her know that I was trustworthy, that I was honorable. That we were all in it together, whatever it was that we were in. I hoped that she had run. I knew my telling would have awful consequences.

I washed my hands and face again. I wanted to have color in my cheeks, so I slapped them a few times. I hated looking sallow and knew that I did, though the mirror in my bathroom had disappeared somehow, and nothing else in my apartment was reflective, now that the windows were coated in grime. I pulled on my shirt to smooth out the wrinkles. It was ripped, blotched with stains. As were my trousers. I finger-combed my hair into a side part but a clump of it came away, so I finger-combed it onto the other side to hide the bald spot.

Margarette didn't answer her door. I knocked again and again, from a whispery tap with the pads of my fingers to a loud, rapping drumbeat. I lowered myself to the floor and peeked through the crack. The bottom of the door was high enough that I could see the legs of her modular furniture. The pieces were in good shape. The wood looked healthy. That was strange. When I was last in her apartment, the legs of her furniture had all snapped off. I rose and walked the length of the corridor, pausing every now and again to listen. No one seemed to be home. I went back to Margarette's and tried the doorknob. It was open. The apartment was spotless. The furniture, the appliances, were new. The walls were clean, devoid of her lithographs, her paintings. This was a vacant apartment. I sat down on the furniture and wept.

How long had I been down there?

I headed to Erich's right away. I walked as briskly as I could up the hill in the punishing heat, lamenting the loss of my muscle mass, my reserves of energy, my camel body. In my prime, I could do forty pushups in one go. I could run a mile in seven minutes. I could throw a discus one hundred and fifty feet. I was lean and sinewy. I was an athlete. All before Uncle came home and sapped me of my strength, of my will to exercise. Either way, I felt reasonably assured that I was not currently drugged. That I was just out of shape. Malnourished.

First, I saw the top of Erich's head, poking above the short border wall surrounding the garden. Then his body came into view. He was in a white t-shirt and blue work jeans. Sweat slithered into the stubble around his lips. He got on his knees and thrust his hands into the soil. He didn't see me, preoccupied as he was. I approached cautiously; I didn't want to alarm him. I wanted to let him work. I felt that a slow approach would give me time to think of a strategy; I waited for the strategy while I watched him. On his knees, he darted around the garden like a frog, spreading soggy-looking dirt from a heavy plastic bag, mulch, maybe, or fertilizer. It really was a beautiful garden, so immaculately planned, so full of happy greens. I could see prismatic stalks of chard, fronds of fluffy kale, waves of scallion and leek. There was a small copse of banana trees, a trellis heavy with ripe, ruby tomatoes, and an impressive vine laden with a mysterious kind of potato. Erich was moving spasmodically. He would never notice me at this rate, so I closed in on his garden until I was standing just on the other side of his wall, watching him from a few feet away. There were half a dozen more plastic bags piled between two rows of produce. When his bag of mulch was depleted, he turned to grab the next one, and that's when he noticed me. His jaw slackened; he appeared stunned. Then he tore the plastic off the bag and began to scatter it around the garden.

"Grab that hose for me, would you, Zelnik?" he said. "By the broccoli."

I did as I was asked. I was still waiting for my strategy to present itself. The hose was stiff and leaking water. No more than a dribble.

"The pipes are all busted," he lamented. Erich moved onto the next bag, shaking clumps all over the garden. Little ivory-colored chips came out with the dirt. They shone like seashells in mud. "Water all of this into the ground," he said. "Do what you can."

I directed the hose wherever he had scattered the dirt. The dribble ensured that it was a long process. Erich kept glancing over at my progress, muttering in frustration. "Come on," he said. "Come on."

"What is this stuff?" I asked. "Is it fertilizer?"

"Yeah, it's fertilizer."

"What kind of fertilizer is it?"

"It's fertilizer," he said. "Keep watering."

"What does it look like I'm doing?"

He paused for a moment, stretching himself as tall as he could from his knees. He came up to about my stomach and looked like a surprisingly tall little boy. "Sorry, Zelnik," he said. "I appreciate the help. You've been a good friend." He sounded sincere, so I nodded and kept watering.

It was hard work, standing out there in the hellish sunshine, performing manual labor. We moved over to the far side of the garden, where the banana trees stood. There was only one bag left, which Erich tore at voraciously until the whole bag split in two and fertilizer sprayed everywhere. Something sharp and significant slashed my face. I bent down and fished the ivory chip out of the soil. It was the size of my palm, coarse, and sharp at the edge where it had evidently been sawed off. I ran my finger around the cut side, which was smooth. Erich saw me examining the shard. He snatched it from me and launched it over the garden wall, well into his neighbor's yard.

"That shouldn't have been in there," he said. "The way it's supposed to work is that they grind out the bigger pieces." He looked me in the eyes and said, "Zelnik, it is simply *impossible* to get good help out here." He laughed, flashing his large teeth.

A still-strong part of me suppressed the other part of me that knew what the ivory chips were.

"Where is Margarette?" I asked.

He looked confused, but then recognition hit him.

"Don't worry about it, pal," he said.

"There's no one in her room. Everything is brand new."

He stopped working and looked at me with irritation; his hands were filthy with soil. "What do you care?" he said. "You gave her up."

"No, I didn't."

"No? Wow."

"I didn't mean to," I said. I felt a rise of panic in my throat.

"You were a little baby at Miriana's bosom," he said. "She asked and you told." Erich smiled. Sweat collected in the creases by his eyes. His white shirt was stained with sweat, too, forming menacing shadows where it stuck to his chest.

I didn't respond. Sweat seemed to fizzle on my forehead, pool in my ears. Erich returned to the garden. I stood there dumbfounded. The ground began to shake and I thought my knees might give out. Erich grabbed my shoulder.

"Christ," he said. He looked into the sky and shielded his eyes. "That's what happens when they pull funding." He pointed into the distance, where little bulbs of fire blossomed in a line out on the horizon. Erich sighed. I'd thought the shaking had been in my mind. He turned to me, his hand still on my shoulder. The longer he left it there, the more it seemed to sear my skin.

"Two quick things," he said, turning to me. "God help me, Zelnik, but I like you. You dumb Jew, I like you. I stood up for you, you know, when they didn't want you. So you owe me. For the future. If we get out of this. They told me you weren't right for Duma. They said you can harness Jewish intellect like you can lasso a rat. But I knew you were a good one. Your parents roasting, your little girl-friend bleeding. A masterpiece tragedy, ripe for the pluck-ing. You should have been a cinch. I shot her, you know that, right? Hallen beat me up about that for months. Got her in the hip. Who does that? Well, Hallen can go fuck himself. I said, let Miriana and me bring him out here. Give us a few months and he'll be on his knees, begging us to sew his foreskin back on. Anyone can be radical-ized. You remember Hallen's class. It happens to the best of them. They just *turn* if you press them hard enough. Some drugs, a little malnourishment." He paused and a ridge of sympathy formed in his eyebrows. "But here you are. You survived that—*thing*, Miriana's thing. That silly rat maze. And it didn't work. Oh, well. *C'est la vie*. Who gives a shit, you know? This whole thing is exhausting. At the end of the day, who really gives a shit? Why have opinions about anything? It's better without, trust me. But you? You should get out of here. I won't stop you. Walk out into the desert. Die out there, alone, with whatever memo-ries you can dig up to keep you company. I don't feel bad for what we did to you, Zelnik. But I do wish you luck. I'll stay here. I'll die in my garden."

Erich turned, his hands at his side. He shrugged in resignation. I saw a tear fall from his eye in profile. He wiped it away and flicked it into the green. I looked out at where Erich had pointed, where the fire had been.

"I put my sweat and blood into this garden," he said. "And now they're going to blow it all up."

Erich had given me a great deal of information that I was trying desperately to hang onto, but the more directly I confronted the information, the slipperier it became, until his disclosures were nothing more than echoes and wisps on the periphery of my attention. With sadness, I let them go.

I did know, however, that I was not going to die out in the desert, so I asked Erich how I could get to the pier.

He turned to me in surprise. "You're farther gone than I realized," he said. "That's a damn shame." He chuckled resignedly to himself, then fished a ring of keys out of his pocket and slapped them into my palm. "Take the scooter," he said. "Drive in a straight line for about forty minutes. Eventually you'll see the processing station. It's the only building on the coast for miles, you won't miss it."

I closed my fist around the keys and turned to leave, but Erich caught me by the elbow.

"By the way," he said. "Did you kill your uncle when you were down there?"

I looked at him blankly.

"Yes? No?"

I said no.

"Huh. Well. Did you see him?"

I didn't answer.

"No? That's a puzzler," said Erich. "He was supposed to be down there. Maybe he melted into the carpet. Maybe one of his comrades ate him." Erich laughed.

# TWELVE

I LEFT ERICH IN HIS GARDEN and found the scooter, parked around the side of the house by the front door, an old, sea-green scooter. I climbed on. The leather seat was scorching. I looked into the side-view mirrors and saw people running behind me, ducking between the houses, screaming. Above them, roaring, nearing, were low-flying aircraft. I tried to remember where I was, where the Agricultural District was. I discovered with horror that I had no recollection of how I had arrived there. Or how I could return. An image bolted forward in my mind. It was the first piece of Miriana's I'd come across—the lamps in the basement of Factory 7A, the electrical current, the latch and the carpet and the halogen light. I could smell the faint scorching of that light. The perfumed memory made me gag.

I steered down the hill, away from Erich's house and onto Reeps Street, which took me past the Fulcrum

## ZACHARY C. SOLOMON

Building and eventually into Beau Gino Plaza. People darted into my path, some intentionally launching themselves at the bike, and I had to swerve to maneuver around them. Heading east brought me through the factory settlements, and I drove down one of the deserted arteries, past the empty factories, past Factory 7A. Here I felt compelled to go inside, so I parked the scooter off to the side of the road, though that was unnecessary: there was no one else around. I opened the door and walked in. The air was still, the guard station unattended. I walked around the boulder of a desk, expecting to see papers, closed-circuit television monitors—but there was nothing. Just the concrete mass for someone to stand behind. I was momentarily grateful that I had not been assigned such a job.

I walked through the lobby and down the hall, following the path I had once taken, passing the rooms where I had been interviewed and processed, toward the factory floor. I tried to push through the swinging green doors but something was obstructing them. I pushed harder, and as the door began to give, an arm came into view, then another, then several legs and feet, clad in factory uniforms. There were people on the floor, blocking my entry. A pile of workers, interwoven on the floor. I pushed hard enough to slip through and tripped on the mass of people, falling among them. I screamed, scrambling to escape, feeling the sensation of being grabbed and pulled downward.

At last I broke free. I noticed that the bodies had holes in them. I ran to the nearest window and tried to open it, remembering too late that the windows opened only an inch or two, and I sprayed vomit across the glass. I doubled over, hands on knees, and tried to control my breathing. I squeezed my eyes shut and concentrated on the neon shapes and lines that appeared. When I turned around, the mass of bodies was still there. I looked down the row of worktables and noticed the people there, too, doubled over, their heads resting on the wood in pools of their own blood. I walked timidly down the aisle and stopped at the row I'd been assigned. My stool next to the window was empty. Beside it was the old man, across from it the young blonde woman. The blood was fresh. His name, I remembered, was Jan.

I ran out of the room, my guilt soaring, prickling my ears and the hair on the back of my neck. I should have been among them, but for reasons I could not fathom, I was not. I sped the scooter out into the open desert, to the east, toward Richard Winger and the sea. It was rocky terrain—desert shrubs, spiky yellow flowers—and I avoided what I could, though several times I crashed and injured myself. My arms and legs were patchy with abrasions. With nothing to protect my eyes, I had to drive squinting against the sand and small rocks that stung my face. The sun grew lower behind me, and eventually I was chasing my elongating shadow across the plain. For a while, there was nothing before me, no visual landmarks at all—until suddenly there was a thin pillar of smoke, curling into the sky. The processing station. I followed the tower of smoke; from where I was it appeared black and green, wavering in the heat. It grew closer, became more diffuse. Then it became several disparate columns of smoke, and the shape that was on fire came into view. It wasn't the station.

Two rows of cypress trees were on fire. The trees formed a broad avenue between them, about a hundred yards long turning it into a tunnel of flaming debris. The smoke was abundant, the wood dying spectacularly. Flaming limbs fell onto the path, crackling. In the center of the avenue was a blackened crater where a bomb had fallen. I steered the scooter around the crater, narrowly avoiding the smoldering limbs.

At the end of the avenue, across from a huge circular planter filled with agave and deerweed, stood a small, square building in the art deco style, two stories tall with white stucco walls and rectangular windows framed by Romanesque columns. Atop the columns were black, diamond-shaped designs. The white paint was soiled, the windows clouded. It was an old building. The area around it was lush with knee-high grasses, wildflowers, Spanish moss dangling from trees.

I left the bike and traipsed across the planter, letting my fingers graze the grass, and walked up to the front door. I cupped my hands and peered through the clouded window but couldn't make out anything inside. No one responded to my knocks. I walked to the side of the building, through the unkempt landscaping, where I could see more grass and cypress trees and the naked desert beyond. A rusted septic tank stood in the shade. At the back of the building was a short staircase leading up to a back door.

I cupped my hands again and looked through the cloudy window. This time I could make out the interior, though it was obscured by the thick mesh of a screen door. To my left was a long work table littered with technological equipment: radio scanners, electronic readers, complicated boxes covered in dials and screens. Beneath the worktable were drawers labeled *MAP DWR 1, MAP DWR 2, MAP DWR 3,* and so on. To my right, a man sat in an office chair hunched over a computer. His back was to me. He was wearing a uniform—green shirt, khaki pants, and a crisp naval visor cap—and was engrossed in his task. His left hand tapped out something in Morse code; his right hand noted data on the computer screen. All around him were papers and gadgets. No one else appeared to be inside with him. Occasionally, he scratched the section of his skull between his right ear and headset with his pencil, but he never took his eyes off the screen. *Shore to Ship,* read the lettering at the top of the chart on the wall, and beneath it were tables of frequencies and ship units. I tried the door but it was locked, so I knocked until he heard me.

The man looked over his shoulder in fright, his eyes wide. Even through the mesh I could see how they were bloodshot. He took off his headset slowly and placed it on the table. Then he stood up and faced me, straightening out his uniform, pressing it over his stomach to smooth out the wrinkles. He arranged his cap with a tilt to the left and pulled his feet together in military posture. Then he made a deft, boxy gesture with his two hands, throwing them forward with a strong bend at the elbows, a salute I'd never seen before. When he was finished, he came over to the door.

It was then, as he was reaching for the handle, that he really looked at my face. He had thought I was someone else. His demeanor changed; now he looked horrified. He took a step backwards and looked briefly behind him, then called out. I could hear his muffled voice through the door. Presently, another man appeared, in the same crisp uniform. They stared at me, discussing something. The man who had been taking notes put his face in his hands and began to weep. The other smacked him in the back of the head and, when that failed to return him to a state of composure, smacked him again and again until it did. They talked for a while, hands and bodies agitated, and I watched with interest the way their backs curved, the way their knees buckled, and the way their fingers played nervously with the air. The late arrival came to the door and put his face close to the glass to take a good look at me. He looked me up and down. Then he smiled. Behind him, the other man fished through the drawer at his desk and took out something that I couldn't see, but I figured out what it was when he held it to the side of his head and fired. I watched him kill himself in the background while in the foreground, inches from my face, the late arrival in his pressed uniform and sharp visor cap kept smiling. I could see his small chipped teeth, the mangy hair between his eyebrows. His mouth alone smiled; tears welled in his eyes. He began to shout at me angrily, viciously, dotting the glass with his spit. He unholstered the Luger from his belt and pressed it to his temple, just as his comrade had done. Rivulets of tears fell down his face, but his mouth kept smiling. I couldn't look away.

I retreated down the steps and completed my circuit of the building. I thought that if I could get inside, then I could radio for help. It was by mistake that I had wound up here. Terrible things only happened to special people, and I was not special. That's why my uncle and I had been on the side of the street opposite the temple in which my parents were burning. It's why my uncle and I survived. We weren't special. I wondered where my uncle was at that moment. I wished him home, in the house on Alizabet Street, across from Mela and Elam, or sitting at his desk by the window and scowling at the blustery street, all alone.

Or maybe he was buried somewhere around here. I was overcome thinking about him. I found myself sitting in the tall grass out behind the station while around me it made a swishing sound in the dusty breeze, brushing against my arms and neck and pushing around the fat odors of the septic tank. Maybe he was down there still. Down in Miriana's world beneath the world. As Erich had said. Maybe we'd simply passed each other by.

I tried the doors one more time. There was no way in.

No way to use the radio.

I returned to the scooter and turned the key, and the bike coughed to life. By now the cypress trees were nothing more than blackened, needleless husks. The beautiful pathway was littered with their charred limbs. Adrenaline coursed through my blood but I experienced it as anesthesia, numbness. The vibrations of the desert floor spread through the wheels and into my bones. It felt to me like something was wearing off, like a veil over my face was disintegrating. I awaited further instructions from my brain but nothing came. In the distance, to the north and to the south, and due east, were craters in the earth filled with smoldering remains. I saw little black shapes swarming the sky. More airplanes, I thought, but they weren't: they were seagulls. A few looped overhead as I drove on. I started to taste salt on the air. It was too windy to breathe deeply so I slowed down till I could and let the salt dot my lungs, too.

The real processing station rose on the horizon. It grew detailed, revealed itself to be like an old sanitorium with regal architecture—an enormous seaside dacha for curing tuberculosis— columns and promenades and wrap-around porches. Its roof was caved in here and there, and an entire corner of the building had been reduced to rubble. Patches of its grounds were on fire. I slowed to a coasting speed. The pier would be just on the other side of the sanitorium. In the foreground I could make out silhouettes and as I drew closer they became the injured, dragging themselves in circles, holding their arms, limping, searching. I drove among them and they looked at me, eyes tracking me across the campus. It was a beautiful campus. The west-facing side of the sanitorium had a grand expanse of manicured gardens, with rose bushes and hedges and graveled walking paths. It was untouched by the bombs. Survivors of the attack sat beneath the cypress trees in the shade, staring into space or talking inanimately to themselves. The air was filled with smoke and seabirds.

I drove to the south side of the sanitorium and saw the ocean. It was calm, the tide lapping gently against the dirty beach. I didn't even know which ocean I was looking at. I drove down a small boardwalk between a sentry brigade of clock towers and got off the scooter where I had a good view of the sea. Several wooden piers extended into the water, laden with crates and containers, with piles of suitcases and other luggage. Moored to the piers were several half-submerged boats, intentionally sabotaged. I scanned the horizon and saw a small fleet of ships, but they were growing smaller and smaller; they were disappearing.

There were people in the water. I watched them swim away from the beach, into the ocean, toward some invisible shore. Some of the bodies floated facedown, bobbing gently in the swell. Human jetsam. I turned violently from the water and the injured huddling in the sand and looked back at the sanitorium. Smoke seeped wispily out of the southern windows on the third story.

The steps that led from the grassy courtyard into the sanitorium were crowded with people. They littered the gabled porch, sitting beneath stone archways, tending to their wounds. The terraces wrapped around the main building in a blocky, symmetrical U-shape, like arms reaching for the ocean.

I tried not to make eye contact with anyone but it was impossible. I was drawn into a mutual gaze with a woman hunched over a pair of splayed legs that at first I was sure did not belong to her. They were so engorged. Her face was broad and pale, and a thin line of blood ran from the corner of her left eye. A dusting of ash lay on her cheek. She raised her hand to me and I took it instinctively. She spoke, but I didn't understand Chinese. I squeezed her palm and let go. She looked out at the ocean and I walked the rest of the way up the steps and into the grand lobby of the sanitorium.

The room was vaulted and the sun shone through the arched floor-to-ceiling windows on the opposite side. Only one of the three magnificent windows still had glass. I walked around the enormous desk at the center of the room. I took in the frescoed ceiling, partially flaked away, of children-as-cherubs angelically sunning themselves, their bodies haloed in beige lights. The whole lobby was covered in ruined old frescoes depicting Romanesque figures, broad-shouldered Adonises in full glory, engaged in shotput and discus toss, their turquoise eyes shimmering, bodies sprinting, diving, fierce at the helm of a chariot, aquiline, oiled, glinting. It was as if the exterior of the sanitorium—the shell—had been built around a priceless Roman ruin.

I traced the walls, mesmerized, trying desperately to ignore the bodies at my feet, some breathing, some still. I followed the walls until they gave way to a staircase bordered by an old, ornamental handrail made from twisting, onyx-colored iron. The metal was cool in my hands; I held to it tightly and ascended the stairs. The second floor branched into several hallways, but before I could pick one, words written on the wall caught my attention. In scuffed bas-relief it read:

**From Power to Power**
Miriana Grannoff

Fresco

I punched the etching as hard as I could, leaving a fist-shaped indentation in the wall. Plaster dribbled out of the hole. It felt good to see how easily her work crumbled. Blood pricked to the surface of my knuckles; I wiped it across the remainder of her name.

The hallways branched into rooms or cells, filled with belongings, or beds, or people. Whatever unspeakable horror I expected was not to be found. Instead what I found were speakable horrors: the everyday suffering of people. I wandered the halls aimlessly, passing others like me who were on their own private journeys, opening the same doors I'd opened, taking in the same scenes I'd taken in. People looking into the eyes of the dying and desperately trying to sublimate what they were seeing. I hoped I was showing quiet acknowledgement to these people, communicating that we were together even if we were apart. Maybe all they saw was suspicion.

At the end of the hallway was another staircase. I paused, thinking that maybe, finally, I had seen enough, but as I turned to leave, I heard an unusual sound: the tinkling of a piano. I listened, smitten—I hadn't heard music, *real* music, in so long—and before I realized what was happening, I was walking down the staircase, following the melodic passage, a descending scale played allegretto, following it step after step until I arrived at a windowless basement hallway. The air was cool, a little humid. The hallway was lined with doors—thick iron doors with small, caged windows. I was afraid of what I might see if I looked through the bars so I didn't look. I kept my head down and followed the music until I arrived at the door at the end of the hall. Now the scale was ascending. The door was propped open.

It was a Bechstein grand, and the man who sat on its bench wore a tuxedo with long tails that swished along the crosshatched hardwood as he played. His right arm draped lifeless by his side as the other danced fingers across the keys. The door dislodged behind me and clanged shut, but he played on uninterrupted. I looked around the room and was stunned by a bolt of recognition: I was inside the photograph. The one I'd found in the credenza, the one that had alarmed Margarette. I was in *that* room. The walls were lined with rolls of felt, and the room was divided in half by a lower section of the ceiling, also plastered with rolls of felt. I walked to the other side of the piano and looked into the player's face. There wasn't one to speak of. He was blind and disfigured, a mess of a body, yet he kept playing.

I ducked beneath the low ceiling and entered the second half of the room where the floor had a downward slant and was slick with oil or grease. The section of the room that had been cut out of the photograph. I couldn't control the tremor in my hands. My foot slipped out from under me and I fell, my body sliding slowly downwards. I caught handfuls of felt and pulled myself back to where the floor evened. I peered down. A gulf at the depressed end of the floor led into the dark center of the earth. A knife of despair split me. They were disposed of while the man played the Bechstein, setting a score to the horror. Their bodies sliding into the pit.

It was an extermination room.

I left the man to his piano and returned to the lobby to sit for a while on the grand staircase, listening to the sounds of woe, the moaning and quiet crying, the bargaining. The air was hazy and thick. It would be better to sit on the beach and wait for whatever was next there, in the surf, I thought. I dragged myself out, through the courtyard that spread between the two extending arms of the sanitorium and onto the boardwalk that led to the sand. The boats on the horizon had disappeared entirely. The air was still; there were no roaring airplane engines. In the distance sat a bank of clouds. The wood creaked beneath my feet and seagulls shrieked from their posts on the railing. I noticed a man standing where the waves reached their farthest encroachment on shore, and I recognized his figure and color and posture as belonging to Winger. To Richard Winger who worked at the pier.

I walked down onto the beach and came to stand next to him. We looked out at the water together, and I felt the heat from his body, or at least I thought I could. I waited for him to say something, to acknowledge my presence. I saw his profile at the corner of my eye as a blurry cliff-face overlooking the quiet sea. At last, I turned to him.

"Winger." I wrapped my arm around his back and pulled myself into his side, nuzzling my nose into his neck. He shook me off violently.

"Get off me, Zelnik."

"What's wrong?" I said. It was a stupid question, but I asked it anyway, hurt.

"Don't call me Winger." He turned to me then, squinting. "My name is Kamwendo."

I stepped backwards, but my surprise felt feigned. It was brutally obvious. I sat on the rough, wet sand, and looked up at him. "Tell me," I said. "I want to know."

He pinched the bridge of his nose as if he had a headache. "They promised me that if I pretended to be Richard Winger and—I don't know, seduced you or converted you, then I could go home." He looked out at the ocean. "I am so stupid," he said. "I actually believed them. They told me, 'Your people win marathons. If his people aren't degenerate communists then they're the ravenous bourgeoisie. Either way, they'll eat you.' I actually believed them. Made me afraid of you. I've been drugged half the time. Down there..." He looked away from me and closed his eyes against space. "I ended my brother's life," he said. "I ended Bakili's life." The surf spoke for him for a moment. Then he looked at me. Vulnerable. Open. He opened his mouth three times, failing to speak. Then he said, "Did you have to kill someone, too?"

I heard Erich's voice in my head. *That's a puzzler.*

"No," I said.

"Okay," said Kamwendo. "Okay." Like it wasn't fair. And it wasn't.

I pulled clumps of sand into my fists and squeezed them into balls. I was having a hard time following. Eventually I stood and took Kamwendo's hand. He shoved me away but I stepped again toward him. I couldn't hear what he was saying; even if I'd wanted to, the words floated above my head like a shower of shredded ticker tape. I reached for his hand again, but this time he swung at me, hitting me beneath my left eye, square into my cheekbone. I staggered and fell on the sand.

"And you?" he yelled, looking down at me with disgust. "You think you're pure? Margarette is dead because of you."

I stood up and charged at him, torpedoing his abdomen and bringing him down into the sand. We wrestled, grabbing at each other, clawing or hitting where we could. I swallowed sand and saltwater, pressed my fist into his neck until it slipped upwards and into his chin, knocking his head back against the sand and rebounding into mine. We rolled off each other into our own injuries, panting. The sky pulsed with my heart.

I listened for a while to the ebbing tide, to the waves whooshing, to the birds, to the groaning of others. I listened to Kamwendo's breath, too, growing slower and slower, returning to equilibrium. "What's going on?" I asked.

Kamwendo's laugh became a phlegmy cough. He cleared his throat and spat bloody mucus that arced onto the sand. "I don't know," he said. "I guess the experiment is over."

I took in this theory quietly. We listened to the tide.

"Did everyone, you know, go down there?"

"Into Miriana's 'art maze'?" He sneered. "Yes."

"Margarette, too?"

Kamwendo nodded. "It was her sister they put down there. Drugged and tied up. Ready to be slaughtered by her. And she did. As I did. To my own brother."

"But what about her pamphlets?"

"It didn't work on everyone. Didn't work on you. Didn't work on me. We were unlucky—we have been in charge of our actions."

"It didn't work on you," I repeated. I looked at him. He was still healthy.

"I faked it. I did what they told me to do. To survive. I don't regret anything."

I thought about the woman I worked across from at Factory 7A. I wondered if she had been faking it, too. All the people I encountered, the concierges, clerks, drivers, librarians—had they all been faking it? Or had they been pulled under by the currents?

"What did they do to her?" I asked. "To Margarette."

"You passed her on your way here."

"What?"

"They hanged her and a bunch of other defects a few kilometers back."

I looked over the ocean at the thunderheads paused in the distance.

He said, "Our lives are rather meaningless."

"Not to me," I said. I was thinking about my uncle. And about Zofia.

I asked Kamwendo what he would do now.

"Who, me? I think I'll sit here until they do another pass. And then..." Wind blew sand against our legs. I brushed it away. Kamwendo didn't seem to notice, or care.

Eventually, I rose to my feet.

"There's nowhere to go, you know. We're six hundred kilometers from the nearest village. You'll run out of petrol and water long before you make it."

"I'm going back to Duma," I said. This made him laugh at me again, but he stood up to shake my hand.

"I'm sorry about whatever I put you through. We're all equally worthless, after all. No sense that I should have had a better lot than you."

"But you didn't."

"Didn't I? I thought I did." He rubbed the dark, wiry hair on his cheek. "I suppose I didn't."

I turned to go but hesitated. There was one more thing I wanted to know. To understand.

"Why did you kill your brother?" I asked. It was an unfair question that I regretted at once. Yet I couldn't help myself. He thought in silence for a while.

"I don't know," he said at last. "I suppose I was moved by the art."

We shook hands a second time and I left to find the scooter. Once I'd returned to the boardwalk, I glanced over my shoulder; Kamwendo had resumed his seaward stance, just as I had found him. The water lapped at his feet. He had taken off his shoes.

***

The scooter was where I'd left it, leaning against a tower of crates on the boardwalk. I lifted the kickstand and started the engine. The petrol gauge registered at about half. I wondered if I could find petrol somewhere in town, maybe rig a compartment to the back of the scooter and carry the surplus there. Six hundred kilometers didn't sound impossible.

I pulled away from the sanitorium and drove into the wastes. I knew I was heading the right way when I passed the gallows Kamwendo had mentioned, a long, raised platform jutting out of the desert. A dozen silhouettes dangled listlessly in the still air. I didn't slow down to identify Margarette. There was no reason to supplant my last image of her with this one. I gritted my teeth into the wind and crushed rock between my molars, trying not to think about anything. I saw blurry portraits of my people in the corners of my closed eyes. They decomposed when I looked at them, as if they had never been there.

I'd been driving for thirty minutes when I pulled over to nurse a cut that was bleeding down my shin. When I killed the engine, I heard the faraway drone of aircraft. I turned in time to see the sanitorium swallowed in flames. Thick black smoke swirled in the sky. I thought of the woman whose hand I'd held briefly on the courtyard steps. She was gone now. So was Kamwendo. Richard Winger with him.

I sat in the sand and poked at the cut. A bit of watery blood oozed out when I squeezed it. The skin was so insubstantial that it looked like a transparent sheet had been pulled taut across my leg. The eggshell coloring of bone bled through. I leaned back, pushing my fingers through the sand, and gazed up at the muted sky.

Night had crept over Duma by the time I pulled into town. Beau Gino Plaza was deserted. I thought that the darkness might mean a suspension of the bombing until morning. I hoped so. There were a few things I wanted to do before then. A few things I saw myself doing.

I drove through the plaza and, against my better judgment, toward where I'd left Erich that morning. I slowed to coast past his house and saw his body among the vegetables and flowers, in the sickly yellow of a patio light. I caught the half-submerged outline of a handgun in the soil nearby.

Erich's front door was unlocked. The house was in disarray: the couch upended, the end tables, lamps, and chairs strewn across the room, splintered, ripped apart. A slash through the canvas of a landscape mounted on the wall. The area where Erich, Miriana, and I had sat God knows how long ago. I followed the carnage through the house, hoping to find anything that would help. I looked in his bedroom, his bathroom. I held his toothbrush in the flat of my palm and thumbed the sagging bristles. The books that lined the bookcases in his office were decorative, hollowed-out and textless. The drawers of his writing desk had had their locks smashed; they were empty, or their contents irrelevant.

I paused in the hallway, surrounded by a mess of Erich's clothes. I thought if I listened carefully, I'd be able find a noise to latch onto. But I didn't hear anything. In the kitchen, I rooted through the drawers and cupboards. His refrigerator was full of food—real food. Actual meat. A rotisserie chicken, a loaf of whole wheat bread, a carton of grapefruit juice. Nothing synthetic. I sat on the tile in front of the open fridge and wolfed down whatever I grabbed first. Even alone, I was embarrassed by my savagery, but I couldn't stop myself. The juice dripped off my chin and over my Adam's apple, sluicing down my chest and wetting whatever hairs hadn't chafed away. Threads of chicken caught in my teeth.

I sat back on the tile and stared into the glow of the fridge. On the door was a collection of jars and vials, of sauces and condiments and dressings, homemade concoctions judging by the handwritten labels. One said *PIG* and was filled with the blood of its namesake. It was half-full. I stood up and opened the freezer, where dozens of other hand-labeled jars were packed tightly, alphabetically from left to right, their labels facing outward. I sifted through them, worming my hand through the rows of cold glass. Erich had written names in black marker on strips of packing tape.

P—Abioye
T—Al-Mufti
M—Baky
H—Budai
R—Chan
S—Fodor
J—Fuentes

V—Hashemi
C—Hite
F—Hsu
A—Jung-Hee
M—Kamwendo
M— Khvalsky
Q—Kozlowski

E—Lazarov
Y—Lee
R—Lemno
M—Mateev
G—Mizushima
L—Nettles
L—Popescu
S—Prentice

E—Rakoff
G—Rolvsson
P—Rosenthal
C—Sowande
E—Stendahl
L—Yoric
S—Zelnik
V—Zelnik

The two bottles labeled ZELNIK were at the deepest part of the freezer. I took them out and placed them on the kitchen counter, examined them in the light. My blood was thick, rufescent—the rich hue of medieval tapestry. My uncle's was much paler, the color of a thin slice of tomato. I twisted the cap off mine and held it to my nose. It smelled faintly like copper and had a cool crust of ice. I turned the vial bearing my uncle's name in my hands, feeling closer to him than I had since coming here. I wondered if this was the blood of people who weren't convinced of the dominant ideology. I looked through the rest of the drawers and cabinets in the kitchen and, not finding anything else of interest, retraced my steps through the house.

I found what I was looking for among the bookshelves in the office: a dossier embossed with Duma's aquatic crest and filled with laminated medical notes corresponding to the names written on the vials in the freezer. The pages consisted of charts of vitals, blood test results, DNA test results, medical prognoses, and various other metrics. With a small thrill, I noted that Kamwendo was AB-Negative. That he was from Zambia. I read that Margarette's mother was Jewish, her father Romani, and that homosexuality ran in her family.

The notes recorded for me were extensive. They included names I didn't recognize, or names that dredged up memories I'd long forgotten—men and women I'd gone home with after nights of music and dancing; pictures I'd seen and books I'd purchased; friends I'd made and social clubs I'd belonged to. My parents and my grandparents and my cousins and aunts and uncles. All deceased. All deceased except for one—I turned the page to find my uncle's name, there: *VASILY ZELNIK*. And all his data. His details. So many of which overlapped with mine.

Where was he? Where was my Uncle Vaska? He was supposed to have been down in Miriana's awful maze. I was supposed to have killed him. They'd lost track of him.

Was he still down there? Was it really possible I had missed him somehow?

I left Erich's house and walked into the dry night. The power had been cut; the minor light pollution was gone; the stars in profusion made a second dusk. I left the scooter and walked back through the plaza. Each step I took echoed off the concrete architecture. *Now* I could design buildings for this settlement, I thought, *now* I could perform my function. As I walked through the deserted streets, I couldn't help myself: I began to design, compulsively, a radically reimagined Duma with a truly equalizing architecture, where all arrivals would be given individual, inexpensive homes that could be expanded, remodeled, or even moved, with little cost and tremendous fairness. A new society where there would be no homes on hills with private gardens—all gardens would be shared gardens—the concrete replaced with organic materials, the light used to invigorate, not stifle, not concentrate, not burn. Windows would open to the full reach of their hinges.

I realized what I was doing.

I was creating a mode of existence that was inflexible in its idealized flexibility, just like Dumanian architecture, only fit to the specifications of what *I* believed was true equality.

Suddenly, I didn't want to design buildings anymore. Nobody should have such power.

Wandering for hours, I turned up streets I'd never seen before, entered buildings I'd never noticed—though I stopped doing that when I realized that the buildings around me, all of these beautiful modernist edifices, were filled with the debris of human massacre. So I did not go inside any longer but kept my roaming outdoors, waiting for the first light of morning which would bring the droning in the sky and the end of Duma forever.

At last, I arrived home to the Crescent, but instead of going inside, I hiked up the hill at the rear of the building and clambered onto the moon-shaped roof to see the expanse of darkened architecture and empty roads.

Not everything was dark. One building still had lights on, high megawattage radiating from its massive, glazed windows, illuminating the manmade lake that rested silently in the night before it. It was the same massive, flower-like building that I'd seen from the car when I first arrived, the same building Erich had alluded to when I asked him where he worked, what he did. He never had told me what he did. An image flashed in my mind as I descended from the roof of the Crescent and walked toward Erich's former place of employ across the undulating hills: an image of silhouettes, of people mingling over cocktails, backlit by the light of chandeliers, swaying rhythmically to the sounds of a brass band, craning their necks forward to make out their interlocutors through the racket; or maybe it was orchestral, the music they were speaking over, maybe it was Mahler—and here I thought of the fourth movement in C-Sharp Minor from Mahler's fifth symphony, not that I was a connoisseur of Romantic music—but I thought of it anyway because it was Uncle Vaska's most beloved piece of music, a spartan, highly emotional, almost irrationally pleading piece of music.

Each time I lost my footing on a slippery patch of gravel, I thought I would go into cardiac arrest. I felt my heart working as it never had before; it felt like end times; it felt like the last hurrah.

Light danced off the surface of the lake. I was close enough to look into the great ballroom, see the dozen or so silhouettes inside. I watched them for a while as they shuttered in and out of focus, as if I were viewing them through an aperture. I could hear the bass of a dance number through the walls. I walked around the lake to the side of the building that was set into the hill, its entrance a long concrete staircase carved into the earth, enclosed by menacing concrete bannisters in which miniature decorative Roman columns had been carved. I stood at the foot of the staircase and looked up. The main section of the building, its head, was an enormous concrete rectangle, above which rose that fabulist flourish. The ballroom took up the entirety of the blockish head.

I walked up the stairs and paused before the arched double doors. I tried to make out what the voices were saying on the other side but couldn't, so I pushed open the doors and strolled purposefully into the great room, then stopped before the small crowd of elegantly dressed individuals, eleven or twelve of them, as they turned to me in astonishment. The music ceased. The room was silent. I took the moment to look at them while they looked at me. Most of them wore black tuxedos with tails or evening gowns, though a few were in formal military dress with epaulets, their breasts covered in medals and ribbons of valor. They all had drinks in their hands; perversely, they looked like they had been celebrating. Some of them were so drunk that they couldn't halt their wobbling.

Miriana Grannoff was among them. She wore a simple black dress and red stilettos. I couldn't read her expression from where I stood. Her face had the melted quality of a Munch figure. She started to approach me, but someone beat her to it.

A rakish man in his forties or fifties with rough blond hair and a matching pencil mustache pushed toward me. He wore a wild smile and had loose, blurry eyes, and he grabbed my hand and pumped it vigorously.

"Well done," he said. "Well done!"

He looked at the crowd and raised my hand aloft.

"Don't touch him!" A woman in a trailing black slip dress threw her hands up in disgust, spilling champagne. "Revolting," she said.

"What difference does it make? We're all the same tonight. We're all glorious failures!"

I snapped my hand away from the man and stepped back. He looked at me in mock surprise.

"Feisty," he said. "Erich picked this one well." He turned back to the crowd, but he'd already lost their attention. They were returning to each other and their conversations, and the music started up again.

"Well, well." His breath reeked as it puffed against my face. He drew me in close, grasping me by the shoulders. "Enjoy yourself tonight. We'll all be bloody dust in the morning."

"Get away from him, Johann," said Miriana. She was by our side now.

"You want me," he said to her, rolling his eyes. "You can't get enough of me." He smiled. Of his two front teeth, one was longer and fatter than the other. "Spectacular failures, all of us!" He shoved me away and reeled back toward the party and the drinks table, roaring with laughter. He made himself a drink and proclaimed a toast.

I pressed myself against the wall and looked around the ballroom. The floor seemed in fact to be a kind of balcony around a large cutaway space in the center, surrounded by gilded railings. I tried to look anywhere other than at Miriana, whose gaze gave off the heat of spotlighting.

"Would you like to see how it works?" she asked.

"Don't encourage him," said one of the men in military garb. This man was much older, a superior perhaps. "Quit torturing the fellow."

Miriana wheeled to face him. "Oh, yes, sir. Yes, Captain Hallen. Whatever you *say*, Captain Hallen." She slapped him on the chin. Hallen staggered but was quick to recover. He smirked, invulnerable.

"Torturing?" she spat. "Brilliant, captain. From *you*." Miriana tucked her hair behind her ears. "I am treating him with dignity."

"It's too late to grow a conscience."

It was then that I realized who the captain was. He was clean-shaven now, no goatlike beard, and dressed in a starched military dress, but it was still him. Professor Hallen. An image flashed through my mind of the photograph I'd once seen of the tattoo on his back—the strangeness of the scene, the cones of light, the frozen swirling particulate, the shadows, his naked torso, and the religious icons buried in his skin with ink.

"Maybe it is," said Miriana. "Or maybe it's not." She turned to me and winked. "Well? Do you want to see?"

I imagined an alternate universe in which I returned to Barnova University for my ten-year reunion, drank vodka and ate hors d'oeuvres with Professors Grannoff and Hallen, and kicked a football around with Erich. I yearned for that universe. I yearned for any universe but this one.

I nodded. As she took my elbow and pulled me over to the railing, I looked back at Hallen, who met my eyes with an expression of—nothing.

"Look," Miriana commanded.

I held my breath and leaned over the railing.

I saw a dizzying vertical drop.

I saw a maze. A vast angular conglomeration with hundreds of paths and chambers. Too many to see. They sprawled out past the viewing area, beneath the building, into the underground.

My eyes danced across the wild pattern of angles, grabbing for focus. They darted, absorbing the dark fuzziness of the lines and the yellow coloring between them. I was aware of the afterimage this was imprinting on my eyelids when I blinked. The contrast cut into my mind. The yellow became bolder, the black darker. I knew what I was looking at before I realized what I was looking at. There was a pattern to the black lines—the tops of the walls—and to certain chambers, certain segments. I squeezed my eyes shut, trying to block out the blazing symbol, the standard-bearing icon of horror perfected, but it was too late: it had burned through my eyelids. It remained, it remained.

I opened my eyes again and saw, as I adjusted to the scale of the symbol, moving iotas like windblown grain, like unknowable dots in transit in the sky that one slowly recognizes as satellites.

The iotas were people.

Lumbering people, taking jagged steps forwards, backwards.

Lumbering people collapsing against walls, falling onto yellow carpet.

The yellow carpeting—yes, I knew it was carpeting. I knew that there was wallpaper on some of those walls. I could see myself down there. I had been down there. I had been an iota among iotas. I had pressed myself against the rolls of felt carpeting made of hair; I had woken up cold and wet and hungry and scared; I had met a man who described you perfectly, a man who said you had been with him down there but the two of you had been separated.

Or the two of you had become one.

Or the two of you had only ever been one. Had been you all along. Deranged, strange, transformed.

Like a hand at my throat I realized this. That I had seen you, Uncle. I had really seen you.

I knew, too, that I had been watched by the people who leaned over this gilded balcony. And that they had watched us, unwitting actors all, in Miriana's masterpiece.

Her face appeared in my periphery. "Hello? Come in, sweet Samuel Zelnik. Do respond."

"He's having a bout of PTSD," someone said. There was laughter.

I gave Miriana what she wanted and looked at her. She smiled and caressed my cheek.

"It's essentially a two-way mirror we're looking through," she explained. "They can't see us through the ceiling, but we can see them. They see a drop ceiling. The mirror makes it look much farther down than it is. A bit of an optical illusion. A wide-eye view." She peered over the railing at her genius, then back at me. "Look around you," she said, "at the beauty in this room." She gestured to the golden quality of the light, the convolutions of the silver motifs etched onto the concrete walls, the power in the atmosphere, the carbon dioxide in the champagne. "Don't you want this?"

"Devoted to the cause till her dying breath," slurred Johann.

I looked back at the maze. Her magnum opus. Her salute to the body and shape of fascism.

"How do I get down there?" I asked. The moving shadows, the lost immigrant souls—any of them could be you. Miriana looked down with me.

A flash of light hit my eye and drew my attention away. The sunrise was reflecting off a silver pitcher on the beverage table.

"Everyone, drink up!" Johann shouted. "They'll be here soon!" The crowd cheered as the sound of aircraft grew in the distance.

"How do I get down there?" I asked again. "How do I get down there? How do I get down there?"

Finally she looked at me.

"You think he's still alive."

I nodded.

"You think you can find him."

I nodded again.

She straightened, organized her hair. She sighed. "It's dawn. We'll be taking our pills in a minute," she said. "I was proud to give this my best efforts. I was proud of the work I did. I *am* proud of the work I did. It's a shame no one will ever see any of it. Such a shame. They think it's a failure—Duma—since we won. Us proud fascists. They're wrong, damn it! It's proof that this is the only way to live. The only way to life." She laughed. "The only way to life. I like that."

Miriana gave me her hand, which I accepted. She helped me up onto the railing.

"If you survive the fall, you might survive the bombing. I designed the ceilings to be quite sturdy. It wasn't easy building so far underground. I wasn't going to have the roof cave in just because of some bad math."

I wobbled a bit and doubled down on my grip. I was scared. I was looking forward to seeing my uncle.

"There's a ventilation shaft on the left side here," she said. "It twists and turns down to the bottom." She pointed. I saw it, a ledge I could grab onto. If I was lucky. If I was precise. "It wouldn't be a straight drop that way. You'd have a chance."

Miriana put her hand on my shoulder and a shock of her thick hair fell over her eye. Then she kissed me on the cheek. "Toodle-oo, Zelnik," she said.

I looked over my shoulder at her. She smiled—kindly, I thought—and then she pushed me off.

# ACKNOWLEDGMENTS

THANK YOU to Reeves Hamilton and Nick Mullendore at Vertical Ink Agency, who found the right home for this novel. Thanks especially to Reeves, for his faith, intelligence, and weird taste.

Thank you to my editor, Christine Neulieb, for her deeply keen reading and editing of the book, and for publishing it, too. And thanks to the rest of the Lanternfish Press team: Feliza Casano, Amanda Thomas, and Aubry Norman.

Thank you to Julia Bosson and Spencer Everett, brilliant and stunning artists and thinkers, who improved my novel beyond measure. And thank you, again, for being my dear friends.

Thank you to those who read the novel in earlier drafts and offered invaluable thoughts: Mandy Berman, Heidi Diehl, Mindy Hersh, Hannah Solomon, and Jacob Solomon. Thank you to Soon Wiley for his cheerleading and guidance. Thank you to Jason Schneider for the horror.

Thank you to the underwater photographer Alex Mustard, who blessed me with permission to use his haunting photograph of a basking shark.

The germ of this novel sprang from reading "Utopia, Abandoned," a gripping essay by Nikil Saval about the history of Ivrea, Italy, originally published in the *New York Times* in August 2019. I wrote most of the novel at the warm and welcoming Bexley Public Library and some of it at the vast and terrifying Ohio History Center, both equally suited to the task and both in Columbus, Ohio. If the novel had music, it would have to be scored by Hiroshi Yoshimura and Inoyama Land.

Thank you to Mindy Hersh and Jacob Solomon for their unyielding support and love. Thank you to Hannah Solomon for her crackling brain and massive heart. Thank you to Judah Solomon and Taryn Brean for their vicarious joy. And thank you to Stellie Solomon, who wasn't present for any of this, but who deserves thanks nevertheless.

And thank you most of all to Mandy Berman, my partner in everything, who inspires and delights me daily, and who teaches me, through her art and her actions, about real, genuine courage and perseverance. Thank you for a life of love and ever-deepening roots.

# ABOUT THE AUTHOR

Zachary C. Solomon is from Miami, Florida. He received an MFA from Brooklyn College, where he was a Truman Capote fellow. He lives with his wife, the novelist Mandy Berman, and their daughter in New York's Hudson Valley.